HICKORY
CURED

Other Books by Douglas C. Jones

The Treaty of Medicine Lodge
The Court-Martial of George Armstrong Custer
Arrest Sitting Bull
A Creek Called Wounded Knee
Winding Stair
Elkhorn Tavern
Weedy Rough
The Barefoot Brigade
Season of Yellow Leaf
Gone the Dreams and Dancing
Roman

HICKORY CURED

Douglas C. Jones

with illustrations
by the author

HENRY HOLT AND COMPANY
New York

Published by Henry Holt and Company, Inc.,
521 Fifth Avenue, New York, New York 10175.
Distributed in Canada by Fitzhenry & Whiteside Limited,
195 Allstate Parkway, Markham, Ontario L3R 4T8.

Library of Congress Cataloging-in-Publication Data
Jones, Douglas C.
Hickory cured.
I. Title.
PS3560.0478H5   1987   813'.54   86-29405
ISBN 0-8050-0383-5

First Edition

Designed by Jeffrey L. Ward
Printed in the United States of America
1 3 5 7 9 10 8 6 4 2

ISBN 0-8050-0383-5

Dedicated to my nine grandchildren, or however many there may be by now, none of whom will ever believe that there were such places as Weedy Rough or the county seat. Much less the crazy people who inhabited them. But listen, sweeties, there were. There were.

Douglas C. Jones
Fayetteville, Arkansas

CONTENTS

INTRODUCTION

It's a pity that what Shanks Caulder says had to be saved for our grandchildren on the plastic ribbon of a tape recorder, because Shanks Caulder does not belong to the era of plastic ribbons and tape recorders. Shanks Caulder belongs to the time of soda fountains in drugstores where you could buy the best chicken salad sandwich in town, olives on the side. The time of hay rides to the lake for kids who knew little more about sex than the mysterious excitement that came with a stolen kiss, square on the mouth.

What follows are some of his words. I had to use a tape recorder to keep up with Shanks, and I really don't think he minded. He was glad that I wanted to put some of his stories into the record.

Shanks, by way of introduction, is a retired professional soldier who started his adult life in the army during World War II. Of course, he never calls it that. To him and his generation, that one was just "the War."

At any rate, once drawn in by the mechanics of the draft, he stayed. He stayed in the infantry for almost thirty years—enough time to give one a few insights on the human condition and considerable understanding of stark terror.

And then, after his soldier days, he came home again to find the only town within short driving distance of the county seat that could still boast of having a genuine, old-fashioned mercantile general store where he could sit on a genuine, old-fashioned wooden egg crate halfway between the cracker box and the yellow rat-cheese wheel on the counter and tell stories about the way things used to be. To anybody who would listen.

Everybody nowadays calls this kind of stuff nostalgia. Shanks calls it sociology.

Well, like the three-cent stamp and the valve-in-head six-cylinder engine, Shanks is a dinosaur. The only difference is that Shanks is not yet quite extinct.

And you don't find the kind of people Shanks likes to talk about too much anymore. They were solid and true. Like cured hickory barrel staves. And like good staves, they had a thick charcoal burn on them.

They were mostly an uneducated lot and few of them were well traveled, at least until the War changed everything.

They had a massive appetite for living. But they faced dying as well as anybody can be expected to face such things.

What was best about them was that they never had to wonder about their identities. Good and bad alike, they never questioned who they were or how they fit into the scheme of things. They knew. It was a kind of wisdom people nowadays go to great universities in search of, and seldom find.

They were proud and courageous and deceitful and selfish and lecherous and sometimes even murderous. Just like the rest of us. And they knew that, too.

They were, in short, one helluva wonderful tribe.

PART ONE
Weedy Rough

1

Halloween
and Other Sacred Events

*It is out of fashion to speak of
flesh-and-blood heroes. And in all of the stories that Shanks
Caulder has told, the word* hero *has never passed his lips. As
he sits on his wooden egg crate, nibbling grainy cheese and
talking, those listening have the sense they're hearing about
people who were a little crazy and didn't fit into any known
mold.*

*But on reflection, there's also a haunting feeling that
Shanks has more heroes than he could count. For a man or
woman to have survived in the era he describes took enough
flat-out guts to warrant at least some kind of recognition.*

*Among the heroes Shanks tells about there was courage,
but, even more important, there was endurance. And there
had to have been humor and rage and compassion and love.
Most especially love—love of just simply* being *in a time that
is now gone, each of them knowing that it wouldn't last much
longer and their lives and their world could be preserved for
the enlightenment and entertainment of their grandchildren
only in the words spoken and the thoughts thought by somebody. Like Shanks.*

Their knowing that matters, you see? Realizing it was

enough that only one person would remember their stories, because most people, wicked or noble, would never get even that satisfaction out of their whole, small, constricted, ass-puckered, eye-squinching lives. A story—a remembrance of colors eroded away, of smells turned to tasteless fog, of touches along the surface of bottomless dreams. The calling back of things past, never to return. And for them, a little immortality in the knowledge that someone would tell it. Maybe the only immortality they would ever have.

When Mr. Hanby Crumb walked past, people always said, "There goes Joshua when he was old and tired!"

I never understood that. After years of reflection, I still don't.

To begin with, I knew a little about Joshua—the one in the Old Book, where they were always sacrificing goats or calves, or sometimes sons and daughters. Back in those very young years, growing up in Weedy Rough, I was like all the other kids who amounted to anything. I went to Sunday school. So

I knew the Book of Exodus better than I knew the structure of government in my native state of Arkansas.

Which was hardly unusual, because almost everyone in Weedy Rough, young and old alike, was pretty vague on how things worked at the state capital in Little Rock. But they damn well knew how Joshua took over the Children of Israel once old Moses had gone on.

Mr. Hanby Crumb had never taken over anything from anybody. And he sure as hell hadn't sacrificed any goats because he'd never owned a goat. Sometimes he was even known to complain loudly to Parkins Muller, the banker, when one of Parkins's nannies worked her way through the fence on Elkins Hill and came down to nibble the fresh vegetables Mr. Hanby Crumb's wife, Rose, cultivated each spring on the hillside behind her house.

Not only that, but every time I saw him, Mr. Hanby Crumb was anything but tired. He displayed more combined energy and spit than all the four or five guys who were always sitting around in the barbershop joking about how decrepit he was and each of them describing to the others, even though they all knew the story from start to finish, how Mr. Crumb had run across town firing a shotgun into the air the first time an airplane flew over, in 1913, and yelling between each blast, "Sky! Sky! Sky!"

That was just before he went off to parts unknown for a long time and didn't come back until the Great War was well under way in Europe. And ever since that trip he'd received, as regularly as sows come in heat, a check in the mail with a postmark of San Saba, Texas, which the postmaster and local hardware man, Bee Shirvy, said was smack in the middle of one big Gawd damned oil field. Bee Shirvy was honest and true, but he was like most people in Weedy Rough at the time. He was sure anyplace in Texas, or Oklahoma either, was smack in the middle of one big Gawd damned oil field.

Anyway, Mr. Hanby Crumb maintained a pretty nice lifestyle on that check. For the time and place. Which is to say he didn't work a lick and could go around doing what he liked best, which was talking to little kids and raising hell with everybody else.

It kept on, that check, and when the Great Depression came like a plague of locusts, any man making thirty dollars a month was considered wealthy because he could walk into Esta Stayborn's general mercantile store and buy a couple of those little glasses of cheese when he wanted to, and not have to satisfy his craving for dairy fermentation with hunks of that yellow rat cheese most people ate, going by 1933 for eleven cents a pound.

Each month, Mr. Hanby Crumb deposited his check in Parkins Muller's Bank of Weedy Rough. But try as they would, and they tried hard, the barbershop gang was never able to get Parkins to say exactly what the deposit amounted to, and in fact he refused to divulge such valuable information right up to the day of his death, when mortal wounds were inflicted on him by four or five bank robbers. And by then Mr. Crumb himself was in his grave six months, having passed on as a result of infected tonsils and other complications, according to Old Doc Caney Jones, who lived in the woods south of the Frisco railroad tunnel, and Mr. Crumb never divulged it either.

Nor did his wife, Rose, because she couldn't read or write and besides that she probably never knew in the first place, Mr. Crumb being as closemouthed with her about his affairs as he was with a total stranger.

Getting back to what they said about his being old and tired and all, I never figured Mr. Hanby Crumb was tired, right up to the moment he drew his last breath. There's no question that he was old. But it was a *good* old, a fierce, uncompromising old that wouldn't admit defeat to anything or anybody. There are those who might say I'm biased about this because of all the chewing gum he gave me. But I say what the hell, if you've got to be biased, do it on the good side.

Mr. Hanby Crumb was a tall, skinny man who wore the

shirts that his wife, Rose, made for him—always white cotton with maybe little figures of red or blue or yellow flowers about the size of a pin oak acorn printed on the fabric. And a pair of seersucker or brown corduroy trousers, depending on the season, always too big in the waist and held up by two-inch-wide orange suspenders. Nobody ever recalled seeing Mr. Crumb in a coat of any kind, even in bitter weather. When there was snow and ice on the ground, he always charged about in such a frenzy of activity that he never paused long enough to consider that it was cold enough to freeze the balls off a blue tick hound, as the barbershop gang put it.

He had a fierce hawk face with a hooked nose that looked sunburned even in winter, pale blue eyes, and a large mouth full of stubby little teeth that looked like they had been worn off by gnawing on tough materials for many years, and the whole thing framed in a flame of white hair. A flame, because it went off in unexpected directions, like the tongues of fire from a burning sassafras bush. He always wore a panama hat, but it seemed like it had a constant struggle to stay on his head, what with all the hair trying to push it off. The hair extended down his cheeks and across his chin and down his neck, even under the ears, which were hidden someplace in the flowing fiber, and the whole thing was set off by the widest handlebar mustache in Washington County.

He never smiled, at least not in public view, and this added to the illusion of anger and frustration that he seemed to cultivate by always moving as though he were about ready to break through an oak door, elbows flapping and feet clad in cracked jodhpur boots slapping the ground like canoe paddles thrashing at thick water.

But even the barbershop gang made one concession to Mr. Hanby Crumb. He had the prettiest woman in Weedy Rough, and some said they'd stack her up beside any of the powdered and scented ladies of the county seat or even Fort Smith.

Mrs. Rose Hanby Crumb was as directly opposite her husband as mortal woman can be. She was small and delicate, and she had hair so black it would shine in the sunlight, and this pale tan complexion with a pink glow across the high cheekbones. And eyes a liquid brown without any bottom. Like looking into a gallon pail of the very best hill country sorghum molasses.

But she wasn't from the hill country. She didn't talk like other people did. There was a little dialect there that nobody could identify, but it sure as hell wasn't city folks' talk, that much everybody knew. She was as common as an Ozark limestone rock and had no pretensions, always smiling and showing her even teeth and always speaking to everybody when she came into town to do her grocery shopping, carrying a little woven straw basket that some said looked suspiciously like it came from Mexico.

"She's got bloodlines," said Olie Merton, the barber. "How she lives with that old son of a bitch is the great mystery of the ages."

Actually, she was a good deal younger than Mr. Crumb. People who were kind said she was young enough to be his daughter. Others said he was old enough to be her grandpaw. Violet Sims, the town's one and only lady of the evening, said it was obscene, an old man like that getting into bed with such a young woman.

But despite Violet Sims being accepted as the best authority around on what was obscene, Joe Sanford, the ice cream parlor guy, said what the hell, Man-o'-War was a lot older than most of the mares he bred. Which was a bit unusual because Joe was a part of the barbershop gang who was always telling bad stories about Mr. Crumb, and it was a known fact that the Weedy Rough Joshua never bought a single ice cream cone from Joe, even during that time when Joe got in some butterscotch pecan and advertised it all over town with little handwritten placards that he nailed to trees and telephone poles.

Maybe a part of the town's fascination with Rose was that they didn't know her origins. Mr. Crumb had gone off on one of his trips sometime before the Great War and returned with her on the evening train.

"Why, hell," Olie Merton said, "when they got off Number Six, she wasn't much more than a schoolgirl."

They never had any children. They just lived together, the two of them, in a small house high up on East Mountain next to Parkins Muller's goat pasture, and each day Mr. Hanby Crumb would come down off the hill, walking through my grandfather's yard, and down into the road below, and then on into town, where he would make orations to anyone who cared to listen, dealing, insofar as I can remember, with the evils of drink, the glory of French kings before their infamous revolution, the robber-baron nature of the Republican party, and the medicinal qualities of lemonade made in a crock jar.

Nobody took Mr. Crumb too seriously. But you had to take notice of him because Rose was hard of hearing and so Mr. Crumb had developed the habit of shouting everything he said. So when he was explaining a fine point of Roman law to some backcountry timber cutter in the Frisco tie yard on the south end of town, people at the North End Garage could hear every word he said.

Mr. Crumb seemed to enjoy talking most to the kids, anybody up to the age of nine or ten. Maybe because they never talked back, being scared half out of their pants with the shock of his booming voice.

He'd come down through Grandfather's yard each day in summer and my sisters and me would be playing and he'd stop and tell us stories about Pancho Villa and Jesse James. We didn't know who the hell Pancho Villa was, but he sounded like a lot of fun when Mr. Crumb told about him. He'd always give us a stick of Spearmint chewing gum just before he left headlong for the town below, and if Grandmother happened to see it, she'd come out immediately and take the gum away from us and say it was probably poisoned. But sometimes she didn't know Mr. Crumb had passed by, being somewhat hard of hearing herself, so my sisters and I chewed the gum and it never did us much harm that I can recall.

One late summer when I was about nine, I was playing in the side yard with Buzzy Merton, a kid my age who always seemed to know exactly when Grandfather had been to the county seat to buy cracklings for his fox dogs. Grandmother would bring out a few of the crisp, salty strips of rendered hog rind for my sisters and me to eat, and Buzzy was there to get a share. Also, Grandfather always brought home a little toy car for me and we'd play fire truck and highway patrol with it in the grass while my two younger sisters sat a safe distance away and watched.

On this day, it was smelling of dust and fresh horse droppings along the road below Grandfather's house and there wasn't a whisper of air stirring. It was hot as hell.

A little while after we'd finished our cracklings, Mr. Crumb came galloping down through the yard, and when he came even with us he stopped and glared at each of us in turn. For some reason he passed out the gum right away on that day, not waiting until after he'd made his speech, whatever it was, and we each grabbed our stick and jerked our hand back quick as though we might be afraid he was going to bite us.

"Well, playing, huh?" Mr. Crumb shouted. Buzzy already had his gum in his cheek and was chewing the flavor out slowly and watching Mr. Crumb with a steady stare.

"I remember when I was a little girl," Mr. Crumb bellowed, looking at my sisters and then at Buzzy and me, with a quick jerk of his head that made his whiskers ripple like windblown water. "I used to play dolls. I used to play dolls all the time. Then one day I was playing dolls and you know what?"

His white eyebrows shot up and he blinked and we all waited to see what, because none of us knew.

"Why, this man comes along and he says to me, 'You wanta go for a ride with me in my flying machine?' That's right."

We were all chewing, waiting, watching his face.

"And I said, 'Why, sure, mister, I'll just sneak off from my ma and we'll go for a ride in your flying machine.' And that's what we did."

Buzzy Merton was standing now, his jaw working on the chewing gum and his hands thrust deep into his overall pockets. He didn't take his eyes off Mr. Crumb's mouth.

"I sure did ride in that flying machine and we drove it all over the sky and I looked down and saw my ma looking for me 'cause I'd sneaked off. Yes sir, we sure did."

Buzzy shifted his feet and by now he was making his gum pop with little moist snaps each time he clamped down on it with his teeth.

"And when we saw all the country we wanted to see, we came back down and my ma whipped me blue for running off like I did. She sure did."

Mr. Crumb bobbed his head and the brim of his panama hat flapped up and down before his wide blue eyes.

"And I never went riding in a flying machine again without I told my ma just where I was at. So don't go off in a flying machine without you tell your ma, and then you can do like me and go driving all over the sky whenever you feel like it. Why, after that, I went riding in a flying machine anytime I wanted to. Yes, I did."

He started to wheel away and go on down the hill toward town, but something about the way Buzzy was watching him made Mr. Crumb pause and glare back, just at Buzzy, as though my sisters and me weren't even in the same yard.

"That's right. I did," Mr. Crumb shouted, only now he was shouting only at Buzzy. "When I was a little girl!"

Buzzy shifted his gum and swallowed and his Adam's apple pumped up and down. He licked his lips.

"You're fulla shit," he said.

I guess a nine-year-old having such language in his mouth defeated Mr. Crumb. He stood there for a minute and acted as though he was having a hard time getting his breath, then he whirled and charged down through Grandfather's yard and into the road and on toward town where he could find more receptive ears.

There were always people who would listen to him. Some of them were just ignorant hill-country men who were amazed at some of the words Mr. Crumb used. Others, mostly the town men, egged him on in his stories as a way of disrespect. You've seen it happen. Keeping a straight face through it all and nodding and later, after Mr. Crumb was gone, thigh-slapping and laughing and telling the whole business to their wives when they got home at night to illustrate how crazy Mr. Crumb was and in a left-handed way proving their own superiority.

The barbershop gang liked the Mexican stories best, because I suppose they could make some sort of lascivious connection with that and Mr. Crumb's wife, Rose. Mr. Crumb didn't give a damn, just so long as somebody would stand still and listen.

It's hard to recall, now after all these years, what I heard Mr. Crumb tell me when I was a kid and what I heard other people tell me that he'd told them. No matter. It proved to me that he had the greatest and most vivid imagination since some of those old Greeks who spun out the tales of world travelers and one-eyed giants and women who sang songs that made sailors crazy.

Mr. Crumb rode with Pancho Villa, so he claimed. He knew the old Mexican bandit, or general, or whatever he was, so well that sometimes they'd sleep in the same room. Mr. Crumb said that Pancho didn't smell too good, but that bad smells never bothered anybody named Crumb.

Pancho kept Mr. Crumb around for the times when he wanted to cross the border and shoot up a few towns. That was during a revolution, or maybe between revolutions, and

Pancho would get restless and call in Mr. Crumb and they'd make plans and then Mr. Crumb would lead Pancho and his men into Texas or New Mexico.

Mr. Crumb said they had a helluva good time. Sometimes a man or two would get killed and that made everyone sad. But Pancho couldn't stay sad long, Mr. Crumb said. So off they'd go again.

Pancho and Mr. Crumb used to sit in some little Mexican town, sucking lemons and drinking beer, and they'd shoot at the chickens wandering along the street. He could cut off a chicken's head at thirty feet, said Mr. Crumb, with his double-action Smith & Wesson .38. But he said Pancho had a hard time hitting a full-grown bull unless he was standing right between the horns.

The first time Mr. Crumb told that one, he was sitting in Violet Sims's kitchen with about seven Weedy Rough townsmen, drinking coffee. The listeners started laughing and Mr. Crumb lost his temper. He ran out of the house, down past the bank, across the railroad tracks, up the hill through Grandfather's yard to his place, and then back down the same way, running all the way and stirring up a cloud of dust. When he burst back into Violet Sims's kitchen, he was sweating and blowing hard and he sat down at the table where the others were still sipping some of Violet Sims's coffee, with maybe a small lace of corn whiskey in it, and Mr. Crumb told the whole story again, word for word, about shooting off a chicken's head at thirty feet, then yanked an old long-barrel .38 out of his pants and slammed it on the table.

There was a rapid departure of citizens from Violet Sims's kitchen. People scattered so quickly that two of her best coffee cups were broken, a kitchen window curtain was ripped off its rod, and a large hole was punched in her screen door. So Violet Sims, waving a cast-iron skillet, ran Mr. Crumb out of her house with threats that if he ever came back with that gawddamn pistol she'd smash his gonads flatter than persimmon seeds.

Having been cast out of Weedy Rough's only house of ill fame, Mr. Crumb went down into the town and stalked back and forth along the Frisco depot station platform, waving the old pistol and shouting vile insults. Nobody had the guts to go out and quiet him down, and even Mr. Harmon Budd, the peg-leg man, roused from his drunken stupor long enough to perceive danger and crawl into the culvert under Joe Sanford's ice cream parlor and stayed there the rest of the afternoon.

After about thirty minutes, Mr. Crumb grew tired of his efforts, and although his voice was still as strong as ever, he silenced it and marched up the hill, through Grandfather's yard, and on to his own home where he shouted out his frustrations to Rose, explaining in some lurid detail the inequities of having to survive in a small hill town where there was nothing but a bunch of ignoramus sons of bitches.

I couldn't have been much more than a tad when Mr. Crumb explained to me how he had been present when they killed Pancho Villa. They counted twenty-six holes in the famous revolutionary. He said Madero came to the funeral and he was president of Mexico then, and after they had Pancho planted, Madero and Mr. Crumb spent the rest of the day eating chili and sipping fermented cactus juice and discussing the problems of the world. Mr. Crumb said he gave Madero a few tips on how to run his country.

It sounded wonderful at the time. A few years later I discovered that Madero had been assassinated a long time before Villa, so I finally realized Buzzy Merton was right. Mr. Hanby Crumb was full of shit. But, God, what style he had in spreading it around! And besides that, his stories about old Pancho got me interested enough in Mexican history to keep me awake when we came to that part in high school history class. Hell, I even wrote a theme once on Pancho Villa and cited Mr. Crumb as an authority, which the teacher bought because she didn't know a damned thing about Mr. Crumb or Pancho Villa either.

Well, there are some among us who can spread it around almost as well as Mr. Crumb did.

Anyway.

No matter how they laughed at him behind his back, nobody ever faulted his courage. The time the Weedy Rough Bank was robbed when I was about five years old, Mr. Crumb led the posse after the four guys who did it. He led the posse by so far that once he had disappeared over the top of West Mountain, they didn't see him again for three days.

Maybe I don't really remember that, but having heard all about it from every direction, in my mind I can see Mr. Crumb waving a shotgun and riding a big gray mule and his white hair flowing out behind him as he charged past the blacksmith shop and up the mountain and on toward Devil's Mountain.

They never did catch those guys, by the way.

Most of all, Mr. Hanby Crumb showed his courage on Halloween. He had to be brave just to stay in town, what with all the kids within miles trying to outdo each other playing tricks on him. Back then, there was no such thing as trick or treat. It was all trick, and some pretty dirty.

One year they put the blacksmith's anvil on top of a telegraph pole half a mile south of the tunnel on the railroad right-of-way. Another time they hoisted Esta Stayborn's stripped-down Model T Ford onto the roof of the telephone central office. And once when Parkins Muller's sister Veda opened the bank after the night of terror, she found the meanest billy goat from her brother's herd furiously munching ledger books that had not been locked up in the potbellied safe. Miss Veda ran out of the bank screaming, holding her skirts and seven petticoats up around her knees in order to get unimpeded action. People who saw it said it was hard to decide which was the most mysterious, the goat being in the bank or Miss Veda's knees.

Mr. Crumb often took personal abuse. Like the year he

woke to find painted on the side of his house in Chinese red paint, "Ass Hole Crumb Is Herbert Hoover's Brother."

And every year, without fail, Mr. Crumb's outdoor toilet was overturned. It was a personal affront, having to go out at dawn after Halloween and push the little house upright and position it over the hole in the ground in time for Rose to come out and make her morning sit. It was a habit with Rose. As soon as she got out of bed and was dressed, she went to the johnny to occupy one of the two holes for about forty-five minutes, contemplating her routine for the day or some such thing.

There was much discussion in the barbershop about whether Rose always sat on one of the holes each day or rotated according to some schedule from one to the other. Unfortunately for the Crumbs' privacy, their johnny sat like a rough pine pagoda at the rising brow of East Mountain, and could be observed from all over town.

"I don't know why the kids bother to turn the damned thing over each year," Esta Stayborn said. "When Halloween comes, it'll just turn over on its own, out of habit."

For a week or two after Halloween, Mr. Crumb stayed so furious he wouldn't tell stories or pass out any chewing gum to the kids. He'd come to town, all right, but he wouldn't say anything, just stomp around glaring into everybody's eyes as though he were trying to determine if they'd had anything to do with upending his crapper.

So one year Mr. Hanby Crumb decided he'd had enough and would put a stop to this business. He loaded up his old Winchester pump gun with number-four shot shells, got his oil stove cleaned and filled, and when it started getting dark on Halloween night, he stationed himself in the privy. Rose raised hell about it, saying the night chill of October would freeze the old man's bones, but Mr. Hanby Crumb, favorite of Pancho Villa, was not to be denied.

Nobody ever figured out how the boys knew he was there.

Maybe they were watching when he went back to the house about midnight to fetch a quilt. Even with the coal-oil stove, it was a little brisk, what with the wind blowing up through the two holes in the rough pine seat.

So Mr. Crumb got the quilt and returned to his vigil, the shotgun cradled in one arm, muttering to himself about vandals desecrating his shithouse, and promptly fell asleep.

That's when they struck. They did it scientifically, so the privy rolled down the hill for about twenty yards and came to rest, door down, and by then Mr. Crumb was wide awake inside his pine-board toilet, and he started blasting, blowing fist-sized holes in the walls of the johnny, five of them in all. And then he ran out of ammunition.

Why the coal-oil stove didn't explode, only God knows. Maybe because He was looking after the man who claimed he had seen Madero years after the Mexican president was in his grave. For whatever reason, the stove only sputtered out, and there in the darkness of his overturned john, Mr. Crumb muttered a few curses, realizing he could not get out because the door was on the bottom and the two holes were too small to crawl through. So he relit the stove, wrapped himself in the quilt, and went back to sleep.

Sometime later he told Esta Stayborn that if those holes in his outhouse had not been cut for pint-sized asses, he could have crawled out one of them and caught the vandals. As it was, he just had to settle down for the night.

Rose, hard of hearing as she was, slept through all of it. But my grandfather didn't, and next morning him and Esta Stayborn and a few other people went up the hill and got Mr. Crumb out of his ravaged privy and positioned the little pine house over the hole in the ground where it belonged.

That rebellion against a system he could not control broke Mr. Crumb's spirit, I guess. He never was the same old hellion he'd been, and after that he stopped giving sticks of Spearmint to the kids in town.

In fact, within a year Mr. Crumb was dead, and mourned by all the people who had looked forward each day to some new escapade they could laugh about and ridicule.

Well, there was one good thing about it. Rose never varied her routine throughout the long years of her life after she'd seen her husband into his grave. Each morning she went out to the johnny for her usual long sit. And she told Grandmother it was sorta nice, sitting there in her crapper each morning, observing the things going on in the town below, looking through one of the holes Mr. Hanby Crumb's shotgun had put in the walls.

I think old Pancho would have liked that.

2

The Law

Shanks Caulder once said that Bat Masterson was his favorite Wild West character because Bat in his late years became what he was meant to be all along—a pretty good newspaperman who wrote stories about boxers.

Nobody cares to speculate on how much Shanks really knows about the history of the so-called Wild West. But it is likely that he became well read in the subject over the years. He had an intense curiosity about anything that happened in the midsection of the country between the days of the horse and buggy and those of metal contraptions that fly beyond the clouds.

What he did read was probably laden with the kind of mythology that has clouded memory of the nineteenth-century frontier with half-truths and downright fabrications. But anybody who has met Shanks Caulder realizes that he knows enough to sprinkle a little salt on much of what he takes in—either in print or from the screen, large or small. Much of the storytelling about the West has taken the same considerable latitude with history that old Colonel Ingram and Ned Buntline made fashionable with the early dime novels.

Shanks once said somewhat admiringly that his grand-mother took anything that was in print as the damn well sure truth, just by virtue of its being there. The fact that it's there always makes Shanks a little suspicious. Had she lived to see it, she would surely have taken television as the Gospel Word. Shanks assumes that virtually anything he views on the tube is questionable.

Nonetheless, Shanks seems drawn to the popular culture slapdash historical renditions of How the West Was Won, each culminating in a shootout in the dusty streets of Ells-worth or Tombstone.

But when Shanks speaks of the only frontier he personally knew, no one need worry about his feeding the myths. The Tall Men he tells about are seldom tall. And none of them, to the best of anyone's knowledge, ever became a pretty good newspaperman who wrote stories about boxers or anything else.

In fact, most of Shanks Caulder's Tall Men were short as hell and had a little difficulty writing their own names.

They buried Leo Sparks the other day. He must have been close to a century old when his heart gave out.

He didn't look very big, lying in the coffin. Even when he was alive he didn't look very big, and somehow when a man comes out of the inner recesses of the undertaking parlor, he always seems to have shrunk, like a downy woodpecker killed with a lucky bean-flip shot and left on the ground. Looking so grand in his black and white and red suit with flecks of gray, but within an hour just a hunk of fluff with maybe some exterior color still there, but all melted away inside.

Not many people went to Leo's funeral. Maybe a dozen, not counting the preacher and the two gravediggers. There wasn't any church ceremony. Everything that happened was at Bethel Ford, a little hill-country cemetery a few miles north of Weedy Rough, where the federal highway crosses the West Fork of White River. It's just a small graveyard, set out in the woods beside the river. It looks like one of those old tintypes you see of burial grounds where Rebel and Yankee soldiers shot at each other a long time ago. So far as anybody knows, no one ever shot at Yankee soldiers at Bethel Ford.

I went because Leo Sparks was part of my memories.

There weren't any flowers except for a bunch of hand-picked black-eyed Susans. They were in a glass fruit jar and the jar was sitting on the mound of rocky soil beside the grave. It wasn't the kind of funeral where the mortuary guy covered the dirt from the hole with a carpet of green AstroTurf to protect the sensibilities of the bereaved. The coffin was mostly cardboard and varnish. There were no limousines, only the hearse, and the guy driving it acted like the whole thing was an imposition.

One of Leo's daughters was there, her and her husband. They came all the way from California and they were driving a new Ford and had on some stuff that nobody in Weedy Rough could understand, like leopard-skin leotards and a peach-pink jacket. They both looked old enough to have been in the coffin beside Leo.

They were the only family who managed to get there.

It wasn't surprising that so few people showed because most of those who knew Leo were long dead themselves. His life had really ended at about the time the Great Depression broke out, about the time the county took over all the law-enforcement functions, and about the time when Weedy Rough could no longer afford to pay even the few dollars a month they'd paid him for years as a town constable.

Leo was from another time. He was from another place,

because even the place he came from had changed so much that in his last years he just sat on his front porch chewing tobacco and wondering where the hell everything had gone. He'd been born, raised, finished about three grades of school, established his own family, seen them scattered all over the country, and then finally died in the same little valley that had been his whole world. He'd survived in his last years on the little dribble of money his children sent him from around the country. And then, at the last, only one of his children had time to come see him put in the ground.

But there was a time when Leo Sparks had been the Law in Weedy Rough. When I was growing up there, I saw him now and then, mostly coming out of the barbershop, chewing tobacco and spitting and hunched over in his overalls and his blue work shirt.

And once, when I was about seven years old, I'd put a penny into this peanut machine they had on the sidewalk in front of the drugstore. It was one of these glass ball things with a slot for a penny and a little lever that was pushed and then out came a handful of peanuts. Spanish peanuts, reddish brown and tasting like no peanuts I've ever had since.

But somehow the machine had screwed up and I'd put in my penny and there were no nuts. So Leo Sparks walked up and handed me another penny. He didn't say anything. He just handed me a penny and I got my little handful of Spanish peanuts.

I guess maybe that was the best mouthful of peanuts I ever ate. But that's only on reflection. At the time it was just another mess of hull-on goobers.

The citizens of Weedy Rough may have hired Leo Sparks because they felt sorry for him. He couldn't do much of anything. He never owned an automobile or even a gun. When he wanted to hunt a few squirrels, he'd walk up the hill to Grandfather's house and borrow Grandfather's double-barrel twelve-gauge, along with a handful of shells.

Leo liked to listen to the foxhounds run, but he never had a dog himself. A lot of times, after the men who did own dogs had gone out to some ridge and lit a fire and were standing around warming their butts and chewing corn beef, Leo would appear out of the night, having walked from town just to listen to the race.

He didn't amount to much. He was just another one of those unimportant guys.

But Leo Sparks was a part of the only feud they ever had in Weedy Rough. Not a shoot-everybody-in-the-other-family kind of feud. Rather a kind of cuss-'em-behind-their-backs feud. It involved the Castleberrys, and it mostly amounted to a lot of hissing. When Leo was sitting in the barbershop and Big Cooney Castleberry or his son Arlis or Monet Scrub passed along the street in the big Pierce Arrow, Leo would hiss, spraying tobacco juice on the bib of his overalls. Olie Merton, the barber, would then observe that there was a perfectly serviceable cuspidor in the center of the room for those with the talent to hit it.

Just about everybody in Weedy Rough would have been glad to develop a feud with the Castleberrys, because, next to Parkins Muller, the banker, Big Cooney was the most detested man for miles in any direction. It was too bad about Mrs. Lillian Castleberry, Big Cooney's wife, who everybody thought was a nice lady. They hadn't seen much of her before she died, just after the Great War. Big Cooney didn't let her out of the house often. But everybody who ever spoke to her said she seemed refined and gentle, a personality that went well with her diminutive stature. The barbershop gang said she died of pure and simple frustration from having to live with Big Cooney and his lout son Arlis and that hard-handed Monet Scrub, who was always hanging about her kitchen when he wasn't in town looking for somebody to beat hell out of or else trying to set fire to such things as buildings and stray cats.

So anybody could have had a feud with the Castleberry
bunch, and maybe a lot of them did in their minds, but there
never seemed to be a solid reason for conflict because the
Castleberrys kept their distance. For Leo, the trouble started
with the Castleberrys' Airedale, a dog that was as aloof as his
masters except on certain nights when he came down off the
Castleberry hill property to make a deposit of organic matter
in the yard of Leo Sparks. Of course, Leo didn't call it organic matter. He called it dogshit and he was always step-
ping in it.

Big Cooney bought the dog for his boy Arlis when the Airedale was just a pup and Arlis was in his late teens. Weedy
Roughers hated that dog, just from the sight of him. Their idea
of good dogs were the yard-type barkers that never bothered
anybody and let people know with their yapping when a
skunk came near the chicken coop, or else the multi-ances-
tored mongrels that roamed the town's streets and lived off
garbage or the handouts of baloney by Bee Shirvy and Esta
Stayborn and sometimes got into entertaining fights on the
Frisco depot platform when most of the citizens were standing around on summer evenings waiting for Number Six, the
northbound passenger train, to come through. And, of course,
foxhounds. Foxhounds were the aristocrats of dogdom in
Weedy Rough, even though none of them had papers like the
Airedale did. Big Cooney had brought it to Arlis from Fort
Worth, Texas.

The Castleberrys had been in Weedy Rough from the time
of the railroad's coming, back in the late nineteenth century,
and Big Cooney's daddy had passed on to him one of the biggest resort hotels in the area. Before and immediately after
the Great War, resort hotels were scattered all around the hills
of Weedy Rough. That was before oilmen and their wives
discovered they enjoyed heated swimming pools more than
rustic surroundings.

From the start, the Castleberrys had never been a part of

the community. They belonged to the class of people that
came up from Texas each summer to stay in the hotels and
terrorize mule teams on outlying gravel roads with their
coughing, smoking automobiles.

The Castleberrys always did their marketing in the county
seat. As far as anybody knew, they had never set foot in any
of Weedy Rough's stores. They never went to the high school
basketball games, pretty much a mortal sin in the Rough, and
they showed no interest in fox racing or the Eastern Star.
Each weekend they rode the train to Fort Smith to attend
Mass at the big Catholic church that still stands at the east end
of Garrison Avenue.

Being Catholic was enough in itself to set them apart from
the home-grown Methodists and Baptists of Weedy Rough.
But there was more than that. The worst part was that the
Castleberrys obviously thought they were better than anybody else living in that part of the country, and disdained any
social contact with the natives.

Big Cooney wrote a postal card to a friend in Fort Worth
during the spring of 1917 in which he complained about the
trials of genteel and sophisticated people having to live among
illiterate, scaly-handed, tobacco-chewing, ignorant hillbillies.
This message was naturally read by Bee Shirvy, the postmaster, after it was dropped into the mail slot in his combi-
nation hardware store and post office, and within a matter of
hours most of the people in town had confirmation of what
they'd thought all along—that Big Cooney and his son Arlis
were assholes of the first water, dyed-in-the-wool, snot-nosed,
big-city bastards. And uppity sons of bitches besides.

In certain parts of the South, mostly the flatlands where
they cultivate cotton and rice and soybeans, a rich man was
viewed with some respect. But it wasn't like that in the hills.
No matter how rich a man was, he had to sit on the sidewalk
in front of the drugstore with the other men, even the tattered and worn ones, and talk fox racing, and spit tobacco
juice, and buy a copy of *Wild West Weekly* now and then, and

act like any other human being with a little sweat on his clothes that made him smell the way a man was supposed to smell.

Big Cooney never did that. And Arlis, as he grew into manhood, sure as hell didn't. So instead of calling Big Cooney Castleberry "mister," they referred to him as a gawddamned outlander, and the things they said about Arlis wouldn't bear repeating.

In Weedy Rough, there were all kinds of Castleberry stories. I heard them from the time I was old enough to listen. My favorite involved the depot tug-of-war.

Arlis had been schooled each year in some Fort Worth, Texas, military academy. When he attained the age of seventeen, which a lot of people had figured he'd never reach, Big Cooney decided it was time for the young stud to learn something about the local hotel business. So each evening during the summer, Arlis drove the Castle Heights Hotel surrey into town to meet the northbound passenger train and transport prospective guests to his daddy's inn.

Along each side of the surrey was a large sign lettered in red: TAXI. Weedy Roughers called it the Pompous Wagon.

Also appearing regularly was the surrey from The Summit, another Weedy Rough resort place. This vehicle was driven by an old man whose name was supposed to be Braxton Bragg. Sometimes he even dressed in a Confederate general's uniform.

Big Cooney Castleberry could just as easily have sent a touring car to the station instead of a horsedrawn vehicle, but everybody figured he wanted to beat The Summit at their own game, showing off a pair of matched bay geldings that glistened like Mexican copper in the late summer sunlight. They had cost him a small fortune in Fort Worth. The Summit's carriage, on the other hand, was always drawn by a pair of horses that looked almost as old and ragged as their driver, the so-called Braxton Bragg.

When a possible guest stepped down onto the station plat-

form, Arlis Castleberry and Braxton Bragg ran for him like
dogs to an open slaughterhouse door, both grabbing franti-
cally for suitcases and hatboxes. For the people who stood
along the station platform, it was better entertainment than
the dogfights to watch Arlis and Braxton tugging on the luggage between them and some poor Texas guy standing there
with his mouth gaped open and his wife and kids trying to get
back on the train, all of them wondering what the hell they'd
got themselves into.

These little confrontations sometimes resulted in a kicking
and gouging match, to the delight of all the Weedy Rough kids
watching and the consternation of the Texas tourist, who had
to see his luggage fought over as though it were Alsace-
Lorraine. In this comparison, Arlis Castleberry was always
the German, Braxton Bragg the Frenchman.

Once, so the story goes, Braxton Bragg grew weary of having his old whiskers buffeted and his ears bitten by the
younger man. So he produced a large pistol from beneath the
folds of his Confederate general's coat. Men, women, and
children who had come to observe the arrival of the evening
train ran for their lives. Dogs barked and a few mules backed
into their singletrees and set up an inglorious racket. The
Texas tourist, his family, and the train conductor scrambled
back onto the Frisco day coach.

As Arlis Castleberry ran around one end of the depot,
Braxton Bragg pursued him, firing the large pistol. Arlis Castleberry continued into the road and turned south, running
uphill toward the Methodist church and his daddy's hotel.
Braxton Bragg stopped at the end of the depot, blowing hard,
and fired the remainder of his ammunition in the general direction of the retreating figure, all without visible effect. Except that Arlis Castleberry did not pause and was soon out of
sight along the steep road, leaving the team of matched bays
and the "taxi" at the station, to be retrieved later by Big
Cooney.

There were those who maintained that this story was one of the myths of Weedy Rough perpetrated by persons having a total disregard for historical fact. But many years later, Esta Stayborn showed me two bullet holes in the walls of the Frisco depot. In fact, that was the last time I ever saw the old depot, because the next visit I made to the Rough, it had been torn down to make way for a parking lot in the middle of the street.

"What happened to the Texas tourist?" I asked Esta.

"The conductor retrieved his luggage from the platform and he and his family went on north," Esta said, and chuckled. "I guess he decided he'd spend his vacation in Eureka Springs or someplace else where they didn't have maniacs running up and down the street shooting off pistols."

It was a story the people of Weedy Rough enjoyed because it made Arlis Castleberry look like such a cowardly fool, whether it was true or not.

But the story about the fried chicken was true enough. Fried chicken in Weedy Rough was almost as sacred as fox racing and the basketball team. And it stuck in everybody's craw that the Castleberrys apparently thought they were too good for fried chicken. They served it sometimes in their hotel dining room, but never at home.

Although nobody in Weedy Rough had ever been invited as a guest to the Castleberry board, they knew pretty well what was laid out there because any number of observers took special note of what Big Cooney Castleberry brought in from the county seat after his shopping tours there. Chicken was never included.

For reasons of thrift and economy, every family in the Rough had a chicken coop. Usually, the chickens were fed a little shelled corn but subsisted mostly on worms and bugs they scratched out of the ground. Not many people had hogs to butcher in the fall, and the only cows pasturing in the hillside lots were for milking. So with a little fried squirrel or rabbit now and then, chicken constituted the major meat staple in most diets.

But there was no chicken coop anywhere near the big house where the Castleberrys sat down to table each night. And often the odor of pot roast or sizzling beef steaks came from that quarter, enough to set every mouth watering on the north end of town. Most families in the Rough hadn't eaten pot roast since Woodrow Wilson's first administration.

Grandfather usually had a hog or two to butcher each year. A lot of that he gave to less fortunate families, and most of the rest he ground into sausage that he seasoned with so much imagination that nobody else could eat it. Except me. I loved it.

Anyway, even though he could afford it, Grandfather seldom bought beef. Maybe that's why a hamburger purchased from some roadside joint that smelled of grease and fried onions was always such a treat. So there in Grandfather's house, like other homes in Weedy Rough, chicken was king.

And could they make chicken sing! Grandmother was a good example. There was fried chicken, of course, but also chicken and dumplings, where everything had the sweet consistency of butter, and roast chicken with cornbread dressing, and chicken pie bubbling from the oven with those golden biscuits on top that you knew had been made from scratch.

Hell, they made everything from scratch then. It was a long time before this business where you open a plastic bag and dump a mixture that looks like limestone gravel into a saucepan and come up with a seven-course dinner that tastes like schoolroom chalk.

So chicken was king in Weedy Rough. Every woman there thought she had the market cornered on great chicken. But Grandmother was an exception. She tried to discourage Leviticus Hammel, the Methodist minister, from coming to her Sunday board after his hell-and-brimstone sermons, even though that was a sure way to advertise how good a woman was with a cast-iron skillet.

Grandmother felt this way because she knew that her husband was so kind he'd offer bread to a man ready to shoot him in the head. And she knew what I did—that Grandfather didn't like Leviticus Hammel very much and on at least two occasions that I can recall admitted that his secret ambition in life was to hit Leviticus Hammel square in the mouth with a cold chisel.

Well, the whole thing was that the Castleberrys not only never asked Leviticus Hammel to Sunday dinner, which even Bee Shirvy, a Jew, often did, but they didn't know anything about how to fix chicken for the table and never tried to learn one of the fine arts of what they claimed as a hometown, a place that had brought them considerable income over the years. It was an affront. It was an insult. It was, as Olie Merton the barber said, shit for the birds.

There were more serious charges against Big Cooney. It was said that he often drove off into the timber looking for stray young women who would satisfy any carnal desire for a few dollar bills. It was said that, even before Mrs. Lillian died, he hired sticks-country women to come in and clean his house each week, and there performed various acrobatic routines in the kitchen with the charwomen while his wife was doing needlepoint in the sitting room. It was said that Arlis, even before he finished schooling at that Texas military academy, was addicted to the same sort of folly. Some of the favorite stories in the barbershop involved Arlis and various livestock, like ewe sheep and young cattle. Hellbent they said.

So everybody could appreciate Leo Sparks's hatred of the Castleberry family. But they shook their heads and thought, Poor old Leo, shoveling sand against the tide, as in the Airedale thing.

Leo was unfortunate in having lived so close to what everybody called Castleberry Ridge, a spur of East Mountain where the brick house stood. Maybe he was unfortunate, too, in having a small patch of what would be called grass lawn. It wasn't trimmed and manicured like the Castleberry lawn, but still, it wasn't a bad little patch of green, flat and kept clear of weeds by Leo's wife, Cora.

So the Castleberry Airedale visited there every night, unwilling to do his doo in ditches or dirt roads or along the railroad right-of-way like normal dogs. And the next day, if Cora or Leo didn't step in the calling card, one of Leo's grandchildren did. At that time, Leo had two married daughters who were still in Weedy Rough with toddler kids. That was before they both flew the coop for California, like so many people did when the dust started blowing in from Texas and Oklahoma.

"So shoot the son of a bitch," Olie Merton the barber said.

But Leo was disinclined to do such a thing. The Castleberrys were friends of the sheriff at the county seat and had a lot of money for lawsuits, and besides, there was that Monet Scrub who was always hanging around and might set fire to Leo's house if he thought the Castleberrys had been offended.

So Leo tried to develop other strategies. He sat up late at night with a dishpan and a metal spoon so that when the offending canine appeared he could burst out with a noise as described in the Book of Joel concerning the end of the world. But Leo always went to sleep.

He thought he might rig electric wires across the lawn to shock the brute, but it would require buying a Delco generator just like the Castleberrys had, because at that time there was no Rural Electrification as there later would be. And Leo could barely afford a new kerosene lamp now and again, much less a Delco.

So he finally decided on the strychnine, although afterward nobody could understand how that was in some way acceptable when shooting the Airedale wasn't. He bought the poison from Esta Stayborn, saying it was for rats, and Esta Stayborn ever after never claimed that he knew the real purpose.

Anyway, Leo ground up some baked chicken backs in Cora's hand-cranked meat grinder—maybe Cora actually did it—and laced it well with the strychnine and scattered it in deadly lumps about his yard. The next morning, as he rose to the dawn, Leo observed four dead dogs on his lawn and not one of them the Airedale.

So Leo gave up. He was defeated. Not by the Castleberrys, but by their goddamned dog. He was town constable of the city of Weedy Rough, population three hundred and thirty-seven, but he was powerless. So he sat in Olie Merton's barbershop each day, splattering the floor and walls with tobacco juice, and could only hiss when the Castleberry Pierce Arrow sped past.

Actually, it had gone beyond the dog for Leo. It had gone beyond anything, except a gut-wrenching acceptance that there were some powers in this world that a mere mortal could never comprehend, much less overcome. No matter how distasteful or disrespectable or discomforting or discommoding.

And as though the damned Airedale hadn't been enough, there was Monet Scrub, who did not defecate on Leo's grass each night—probably because he never thought of it—but who would stalk about the town as though he were a decent citizen and shout that the people of Weedy Rough and their representative of order were all gnats on a pile of cowshit.

Usually such pronouncements were made when Grandfather or Esta Stayborn was not present because these two men were the pillars of the community, and I have always suspected that Monet Scrub thought Grandfather could dissolve him into a mass of gluck, like when a housewife puts salt on a slug. But the pronouncements were made, and almost always when Leo Sparks was within hearing.

Monet's mother had been a housecleaner for the Castleberry family. It went back a long time. She wasn't a cook or a chambermaid or anything that required a faint touch of in-

telligence. She was just a charwoman and general pick-
upper.

Some of the old-timers who knew her family said she was
a little addled, a little windblown in the head, because she
came from a family far out in the backwoods where the in-
breeding would curl the hair of a sexual behavior researcher
at the University of Indiana. Of course, that was a long time
before researchers at the University of Indiana or anywhere
else were putting into public print things that had to do with
stuff as raunchy as incest.

But the old-timers in the hills knew all about incest, even
though they'd never had the opportunity to read about it in
some scholarly journal. I can recall hearing conversations I
wasn't supposed to hear, like when one of the old-timers
would tell about some family way out in the sticks where the
daddy of the clan delivered his own daughter's baby, whom
he had sired, and afterwards carried the still-bloody newborn
into some timbered hollow and knocked it in the head with a
rock.

Not that all families who lived in the backwoods carried on
like that, but a few did, according to the old-timers. And Lula
Scrub, they said, was a member of such a bunch but had
somehow escaped the rock.

Nobody knew if Monet Scrub was aware of his clouded
genealogy, but they said that even if he was, he likely didn't
give a damn. In fact, they said, if he thought his grandpaw and
his great-grandpaw were one and the same rusty-necked timber cutter, it would give him one helluva big laugh.

Anyway, for years the townspeople would see Lula Scrub
walking in from her daddy's hillside farm each morning just
after first light in summer, and they assumed she did the same
thing in winter, arriving while it was still dark, and in either
case to perform her duties in the brick house on Castleberry
Ridge. Then, toward the end of the day, they would see her
walking back into the woods along the gravel road that led off
toward Devil's Mountain. It didn't make any difference if the

weather was sweltering hot or there was snow on the ground and the oaks along the way were coated with ice, Lula always walked in each day to help keep Big Cooney's house in order and back into the wilderness again each night.

Even when it became apparent that Lula was heavy with child, the trek into town and back again each day continued right up to the day she gave birth in one of the Castleberry bedrooms. Everybody said it was likely Mrs. Lillian, then about to deliver herself of Arlis, who had insisted that the faithful Lula have her baby in some sort of civilized surroundings and with Old Doc Jones in attendance.

Then Lula Scrub became a stay-in employee on Castleberry Ridge. And not just a stay-in until she had recovered from the delivery, which actually took about two hours, but permanently, along with her baby boy, whom Old Doc Jones said had the biggest head he'd ever seen on a newborn child. Old Doc Jones further informed the town at large that Lula had named the baby Monet because she'd heard that Monet, Missouri, was a stop on the Frisco line for northbound Number Six passenger train and was in a foreign land and they had electric lights and indoor toilets in every home there.

The arrangement at the brick house went on for three years, until one day, in the heat of summer, Lula Scrub, carrying a new suitcase that everyone figured was stuffed with Montgomery Ward clothes and shoes, came down off Castleberry Ridge and walked through the town past the Frisco depot, out the West Mountain road toward Devil's Mountain, and never came back.

And left the boy, who was growing up alongside Arlis Castleberry, a situation Mrs. Lillian obviously not only approved of but maybe even demanded, because the same day that Lula went back home, a woman wearing a high-collar dress that might have been in style for President McKinley's inaugural ball arrived from Texas on Number Six and took up duties in the brick house as governess for the two boys.

Esta Stayborn told me later, "It was more than just being

kind to a little boy faced with the prospect of life in the backwoods, like Lula's baby was. It provided a built-in compan-
ion for Arlis. Because sure as hell, Mrs. Lillian knew that no
Weedy Rough kid would ever go up there to Castleberry
Ridge to play with him.''

Weedy Roughers could understand Lula Scrub walking off
and leaving her son because after all, they said, she was crazy
as hell. And those same Weedy Roughers took note of the fact
that Lula's daddy suddenly became relatively prosperous.
Two weeks after Lula took her final walk from the brick
house, her father drove his log wagon into the Frisco tie yard
drawn by two large roan mules that Olie Merton said were
worth at least sixty dollars each. And the old man had enough
cash in his pockets to visit Esta Stayborn's general mercantile and buy a half dozen cans of corned beef and two pairs
of apple-red flannel underwear.

So Arlis Castleberry and Monet Scrub grew up together.
The only schooling they had until Arlis was old enough to be
shipped off to the Fort Worth military academy came at the
hands of the governess. Weedy Roughers said this was not
Mrs. Lillian's idea. It was Big Cooney's. Because in the first
place, Big Cooney wouldn't allow his son to be contaminated
by the Weedy Rough public school, and in the second knew
that any time Arlis Castleberry set foot on the local school-
yard, every boy in sight would be lining up to whip his ass.

But finally Arlis Castleberry was sent off for a disciplined
education and the governess went back to wherever it was she
had come from and that marked the end of any schooling
Monet Scrub ever had.

Monet always waited out the winter, lying about in the
brick house on Castleberry Ridge or else helping to paint
rooms in the Castle Heights hotel. Then Arlis would arrive
home for the summer, usually wearing a pair of cowhide
jodhpur boots and a wide-brim straw hat, and the two of them
would become once more as close as two lice in the same

head of hair. Each year growing. Each year melded together. Each year getting bigger and meaner and learning to drive one of Big Cooney's automobiles and consorting with the young men who were guests in Big Cooney's hotel, all of them charging around the county in big touring cars, kicking up dust and drinking grain alcohol laced with essence of juniper and calling it gin and terrorizing the local wildlife.

And then Mrs. Lillian was gone, and with her died any prospect for friendly or understanding accommodation between her son and the rest of Weedy Rough. There hadn't been much chance of such a thing before they took her off to a Fort Smith hospital where she died and then was buried in a graveyard there, and afterward there was no chance at all.

In 1927, with Arlis already graduated from his Fort Worth military academy and Monet the acknowledged brute and bully of the whole county, Big Cooney went to join Mrs. Lillian. Well, maybe not. Leo Sparks said that maybe they went in different directions, and in fact if Big Cooney didn't go square to hell, along with his dog when the dog's time came, there was no justice in the system.

It was the flu, a few holdover bugs from the big epidemic associated with the Great War. When Big Cooney came down with it, Arlis and Monet took him to Fort Smith on the southbound passenger train and he lasted three days in one of the St. Edward's or St. Vincent's or St. whatever-it-was hospitals and then they buried him under a massive gray granite headstone that probably cost more than most houses in Weedy Rough would, and only a short distance from the grave of Mrs. Lillian. It was the most expensive, exclusive, well-mown graveyard in western Arkansas, where there were rows of cedar trees and a cast-iron fence all around and a sandstone belltower from which issued various heavenly chime sounds each evening at six o'clock and where the cardinals always nested in the boxwood hedges in the summertime.

Everybody in Weedy Rough reckoned that Arlis Castleberry would run out the season as the owner now of Castle
Heights, and then sell and move on to fields more fleshy.
They hoped he'd take Monet Scrub with him. At least part of
that expectation was realized.

Arlis operated the hotel through the rest of the summer of
Big Cooney's death. And then, on almost the exact night the
last Texas guest departed, the hotel caught fire and burned to
the ground. Some of the women in the Ladies' Aid Society
said it was a stroke of God against transgressors. But the
barbershop gang knew better.

There arrived from Dallas a mousy little man with a derby
hat and a walking stick and a fake pearl stuck in his necktie,
and he poked about in the ashes of the late Castle Heights
hotel and after two days, having stayed in The Summit, where
Braxon Bragg must have been gloating, boarded the southbound train and went back to Texas. And in two weeks, as
reported by Bee Shirvy the postmaster, a registered letter arrived, addressed to one Arlis Castleberry. Whereupon Arlis
went to the county seat in his newest car, which happened
then to be a Starr, and made a visit to the bank where his
daddy Big Cooney had always done financial business. He
returned to Weedy Rough and settled in with Monet Scrub at
the brick house on Castleberry Ridge and commenced three
years of drinking and cooking steaks on a thing in the yard he
called a barbecue pit and entertained guests of the opposite
gender on a weekly basis, the guests having been collected in
his late-night forays to Tulsa and Muskogee and other Oklahoma high spots.

Getting insurance on a Weedy Rough hotel was not easy.
But Big Cooney had obviously paid out a lot of money for just
that, and when the Big Bug got him, Arlis cashed in on it.

I've thought a lot about that fire in the years since it happened. Maybe Arlis Castleberry had a better idea of what was
about to happen than anybody else. And what was about to

happen, namely the Great Depression, would wipe out the hotel business in Weedy Rough. Besides, there were a growing number of other places with more to offer, like golf courses where you didn't have to fight the squirrels for your ball. So rather than struggle against the tide, maybe Arlis Castleberry just decided to torch it, or at least have Monet Scrub do it, and get the most out of it that he could.

Or maybe Arlis was too lazy to run a hotel anyway. Or maybe he liked to watch fires burning in the night.

Whatever, Arlis Castleberry and Monet Scrub settled into the brick house and sat like a growing wart on the north end of Weedy Rough. They never patronized its stores. They never spoke to its people in any kind of "howdy" fashion, but only with slurs and obscenities. They never ate an ice cream cone from Joe Sanford's place. They never had a cherry Coke from Dick Page's drugstore fountain. They never went to the gym to see the Weedy Rough Chipmunks basketball team beat hell out of West Fork. And with the hotel in ashes, they were never even a part of the community to the extent that Big Cooney had been. At least with Big Cooney there was a place that attracted Texas trade and brought in some money to the town.

During summer months, once each week, a bob truck came down from the county seat with half a dozen guys to manicure the lawn around the brick house. Leo Sparks could sit on his front porch and watch all day as Arlis and Monet came from the brick house with bootleg beer and whiskey and passed it around to the workers, and everybody laughing and telling jokes and throwing sticks for the Airedale to retrieve. It always took that county seat yard gang most of the day to do a job that Leo knew he could have done in two hours, alone and without the bootleg juice.

Then the Airedale died, of old age. It was the same year they had the St. Valentine's Day massacre in a Chicago garage. Everybody knew about that because the Sunday *Den-*

ver Post and the *Chicago Tribune,* the two newspapers a lot
of people in the Rough bought, played it very large.

Well, sometimes people didn't buy the papers. They just
stood in Dick Page's drugstore and read them and then slipped
them back on the rack beside *The Shadow* or *Rangeland Ro-
mances* or *Flying Aces* or some other such pulp magazine.
Then sometimes, because of guilt, would go over to the gray
marble soda-fountain counter and throw down a nickel and
say, "Gimme a lemon Coke," or some such thing. The nickel
made up for sneaking a look at Dick Page's newspapers that
reported folks being sliced up by machine guns in Chicago or
frying in an electric chair at Sing Sing, like Ruth Snyder.
Reading stuff like that was worth the price of a lemon Coke.

I can recall Grandfather always took the *Chicago Tribune*
because it had the best funny papers. It arrived in Weedy
Rough each Thursday morning on the southbound Frisco
passenger train. Of course, the news stuff wasn't what could
be called hot-off-the-presses, but who the hell cared about the
most recent escapades of some redneck politician from the
Louisiana swamps named Huey Long when Barney Google
was in a tight fix?

My old man, who was then still in the good graces of my
mother, preferred the *Denver Post* because each Sunday edition had a full-page, full-color reproduction of a painting of
some guy doing Wild West things like panning gold or shooting at Indians. The old man liked anything dealing with the
shooting of Indians, because once, when he was working the
oil fields around Bartlesville, Oklahoma, a big Osage, drunk
as sin, had insisted on smoking the old man's pipe and even
tried to take it right out of his mouth, which resulted in a small
scuffle that the old man lost. Anyway, I think he liked all
those blood-red headlines in the *Post.*

Came the time when those newspapers were reporting the
stuff that would affect almost everybody in the Rough. Like
the Japs taking a big hunk of China and renaming it Manchu-

kuo, and a Bonus March on Washington by a lot of veterans who had fought in the Great War and the whole thing broken up by federal troops under the eye of a general named MacArthur, and a guy named Hitler becoming the big man in Germany, and Franklin D. Roosevelt being elected President and starting to talk to the nation on the radio.

It took a while before some of those things had any effect, but some came quickly, like the Blue Eagle New Deal, a part of which was the WPA. That meant Work Projects Administration, but most people called it "We Piddle Around." One of the things they did was build new outhouses for people who didn't have indoor plumbing, and in Weedy Rough that included everybody except Arlis Castleberry, whose brick house had had inside pipes since Big Cooney's youth.

These were classy outhouses with concrete foundations. For that and other vague reasons few of them could explain, people had taken Franklin D. Roosevelt to heart and they never let him go. In fact, they called their new hard-bottomed privies Roosevelts, maybe the finest accolade ever paid a United States President.

Everybody liked the new crappers except the kids, because these johns were bolted to the concrete bases and couldn't be overturned on Halloween.

Another thing that had immediate effect was passage of the Twenty-first Amendment to the Constitution, which repealed Prohibition. Now a man—or a woman, for that matter—could do all the same kind of drinking they'd been doing all along but without breaking the law.

Two people who took advantage of Repeal in obvious and obnoxious manner was Arlis Castleberry and Monet Scrub. Everybody else took it with a shrug, saying what the hell, you can still get good moonshine from Violet Sims, the town's wicked lady, and you can still get beer in the machine shop across the street from the bank. Just like you always could.

But now Arlis and Monet seemed bent on flaunting their

wealth even more than they had before by tooling around in
their new car, a canary-yellow Model A Ford convertible
roadster, waving bottles with green stamps on the top that
indicated they were one hundred proof, bottled in bond, and
far beyond the economic reach of anybody else except Esta
Stayborn and Grandfather, neither of whom drank anyway.

It was an affront to the peace and dignity of the Rough, said
Olie Merton, and proved what he'd always claimed, that Monet Scrub was the kind of insect who would eat anything
that didn't eat him first, and Arlis Castleberry provided the
ketchup.

Everybody in the barbershop gang nodded in agreement,
although it was doubtful they understood the full import of the
metaphor and maybe Olie didn't either. Anyway, this new
method of Arlis and Monet for rubbing Weedy Rough's nose
in its helplessness at the hands of unbridled, uninhibited,
onerous public behavior that seemed calculated to corrupt the
morals of children and defy the conventions of good, God-
fearing Methodists, not to mention Baptists, brought on the
final confrontation between the two and Leo Sparks, the Law
of Weedy Rough.

It was mid-July, and all afternoon the leaves on the sycamores and oaks were turned belly-up, exposing their white
undersides. A sure sign of rain, Grandmother said. By late
afternoon there were vicious-looking black clouds rolling in
over West Mountain, straight out of Oklahoma. And the flies
were biting like sharks.

I was spending that week with my grandparents and we'd
all gone down into town to watch Number Six come in, and
after the train had pulled out for Missouri, we went into Joe
Sanford's ice cream parlor and had fresh strawberry sun-
daes. Then we trooped back up East Mountain to Grandfather's house and sat down in front of his battery-powered
radio to listen to "Amos 'n' Andy." Or maybe it was "Lum 'n'
Abner." Or if it was Saturday night, it was "The National

Barn Dance'' out of Chicago. Grandfather never liked any of
that Nashville bunch and ''The Grand Ole Opry.''

Anyway, with thunder beginning to echo across the hills
from the direction of Devil's Mountain, there was the sound
of footsteps on the long porch at the front of the house.
Grandfather went out to see who was calling, and I listened
from an open window. It was Leo Sparks, and I heard exactly what he said.

''Noah,'' he said, ''I'd like to borrow that pistol of yours.
There seems like a little trouble downtown.''

So Grandfather got the gun from his bedroom closet and a
handful of ammunition, and Leo put both under his coat and
said he was much obliged and left. It gave me big goose
bumps.

This gun was just a little Colt double-action revolver
chambered for .38 shorts. It didn't amount to much in a community that leaned heavily toward .45s. I have never understood why Grandfather even had it. If a weasel got into the
hen house, he'd always grab the shotgun.

Anyway, Leo Sparks walked back into town, and later I
heard all about what happened there. Olie Merton and Joe
Sanford and Dick Page and about everybody who ran a business in Weedy Rough were just leaving their places and saw
it. And for the rest of their lives, they told it.

After the northbound train whistled and pulled out, all the
people who had gathered went away, as they always did,
shouting to one another up the hills and valleys to ''come see
us.'' The street was empty and there were no longer any cars
or wagons at the Frisco depot platform. It was the summer
gloaming, with the smell of coalsmoke locomotive still in the
valley and people like Esta Stayborn putting the padlocks on
their doors. That's when the yellow roadster, canvas top
down, roared into the street in front of the drugstore, made a
sharp turn toward the depot platform, hit a rain barrel that
always stood at the northeast corner of the Frisco station and

shattered it, sending staves and hoops in a mangled scatter, and threw up dust and gravel as it came to a stop head-on at the railroad platform.

Arlis Castleberry was driving. Beside him was some young woman nobody had ever seen before, and in the rumble seat were Monet Scrub and another young woman.

They were making a lot of obscene noise. And as soon as the roadster was fully stopped, Arlis and Monet leaped out and jumped up on the depot platform and started doing a little dance and Arlis had a quart bottle in his hand and the two women established themselves in the rumble seat, standing up, and all of them began to sing a very dirty song about some French lady who bought Vaseline by the case lot.

What was maybe worse, they were all wearing bathing suits, wet from a recent dip in some creek pool, and the clinging woolen material against naked skin left very little to the imagination.

Weedy Rough, Arkansas, was not Atlantic City, New Jersey, and didn't want to be, and people running around very nearly buck naked on a railroad platform drinking from bottles and shouting words close to real dirty was viewed somewhat like the second coming of the Black Plague. It was outright blasphemy.

So, standing under the awning over the sidewalk in front of the barbershop, Olie Merton said to Leo Sparks, "Leo, you gotta do something about this."

That's when Leo came to Grandfather's for the pistol. And gave me the goose pimples.

Maybe Olie Merton and Joe Sanford and the others thought Leo was running away, but they soon found out differently, and it didn't matter that Leo took twenty minutes or so to arm himself, because apparently Arlis Castleberry and his group had come prepared to make a party that would last a considerable long time right there on the Frisco platform in front of every citizen of Weedy Rough who had the stomach to watch.

Arlis Castleberry was cavorting along the platform in front of his new yellow roadster, and Joe Sanford said he looked like a Russian toe-dancer, although nobody ever questioned Joe Sanford's knowledge of such things. The two strange women continued to stand in the rumble seat of the car, waving bottles and screeching words that were supposed to be known only to railroad section hands or penitentiary inmates or regular-army first sergeants. Monet Scrub was prancing up and down the platform, bellowing challenges to the general population.

"The son of a bitch is crazy," said Olie Merton, which everyone already knew.

Then Leo Sparks came down off the hill with Grandfather's pistol under his coat. Of course, nobody knew he had the gun. He was just little Leo Sparks with tobacco juice around his lips and an old sweat-stained hat that looked like gray cardboard and a coat too big and feet in cracked leather shoes he'd worn for ten years. And just walking along with his toes pointed in strange directions with each step, as though he wasn't sure whether he wanted to go left or right, and his jaw working on the cud. When Olie Merton saw him going toward the depot platform, he said, "Oh, Christ! I never should have told him he oughta get involved in this."

As Leo passed the corner of the depot, he bent and took up one of the staves from the destroyed barrel and held it in his left hand, down low behind his leg so nobody could see it. He stepped onto the station platform and moved toward the yellow roadster. The dancers didn't see his approach, or else ignored it. He was within ten feet of them before Arlis Castleberry threw up his hands, one still holding a quart bottle of bonded whiskey, and shouted in mock terror, "Oh, my gracious! It's the law, it's the law, come to eat us up!"

The two women squealed with laughter and clapped their hands and jumped up and down in the rumble seat. And the men of Weedy Rough standing along the sidewalk across the street behind them observed how swimming suits creep up and a few later were large enough to admit that they didn't really give a damn what happened to Leo Sparks, as long as those two strange women kept leaping.

Monet Scrub turned to face Leo and there was a wicked, evil grin on his face. Leo was within three feet of him when Monet swung a massive right fist and Leo just seemed to fade under it so the blow went harmlessly over his head, and at the same time delivered a short, chopping blow with the barrel stave so the edge of hard hickory wood sliced across Monet Scrub's right shin.

Monet squealed and started hopping around, holding his bruised shin and Leo hit him again, this time with the flat of the stave across the nose, and blood splattered down Monet's hairy chest and onto his navy-blue woolen swimming suit. And Leo hit him once more, again with the edge of the stave and this time on the knee of Monet's one remaining serviceable leg. Monet went down, thrashing about on the depot platform, kicking up cinders and gravel and screaming, holding both legs now.

"The son of a bitch busted my kneecap!"

Arlis Castleberry and the two women in the rumble seat stood frozen, as motionless as Lot's wife after she'd looked back. Leo turned from Monet Scrub as though he had ceased to exist, and pointed the barrel stave at Arlis.

"Arlis," Leo said, "you get Monet back in that car and you take him and these women and you get on home and dried off and into some decent clothes or I'm going to ruin your new roadster."

Arlis Castleberry drew himself up and his cheeks puffed out and he lifted the bottle as though it might be a club.

"Who do you think you are, telling me what to do?" he shouted, and the men across the street along the sidewalk said he was foaming a little at the mouth.

Leo reached inside his coat with his left hand and pulled out Grandfather's pistol and pointed it at the radiator of the yel-

low roadster and pulled the trigger. Arlis lowered the bottle
and stood there on the station platform half bent, leaning as
he might have done just before diving into the swimming hole,
and watched as liquid began to spurt from the puncture in his
radiator.

"My God, you've shot my car!" he wailed.

"I'm fixin' to shoot it some more," Leo said.

"Jesus H. Christ!" Arlis yelled, and dropped the bottle and
ran over to Monet, who was still pawing at his legs and
shouting observations concerning Leo Sparks's ancestry.
Arlis took the bigger man under each arm and dragged him
off the platform and boosted him into the front seat of the car.

"He done busted my gawddamned kneecap!" Monet was
shouting.

Arlis ran around the car and got in under the steering wheel,
and the two women were still standing in the rumble seat,
mouths open.

"I'll get you, you bastard!" Arlis yelled, and Leo pointed
the pistol and fired again, shattering the right headlight in a
shower of glass, and the slug ricocheted down into the right
front tire and it gave a little puff of sound like a quickly ex-
pelled breath and sagged, flat as Lottie's sock, so Olie Merton reported.

Arlis threw the Ford into reverse and backed away from the
platform with such a jerk that one of the women standing in
the rumble seat was thrown forward onto Monet Scrub, who
started hitting her and trying to get from beneath her and getting his nose blood all over her as she started screaming for
help.

The other woman, still half-standing in the rumble seat,
grabbed a handful of the folded canvas top and hung on as
Arlis wheeled the car around in a cloud of dust and gravel,
grated into first gear, and headed north. The car was jerking
and bounding along on the flat tire, and now that the water
pump was working, the juice spurted from the hole in the radiator in a nice little stream. As the car swept past them—

running like a three-legged dog, so Joe Sanford said—the men
standing along the sidewalk could see that tears of rage and
frustration were streaming down Arlis Castleberry's face.

Everything had happened so fast. Olie Merton and Joe
Sanford and the rest were still standing along the sidewalk
across the street from the depot platform, motionless and silent and watching Leo Sparks, still looking small and maybe
a little forlorn, staring down at the still-half-full bottle of
bonded whiskey that Arlis Castleberry had dropped.

It started to rain about then. And there was thunder and
flashes of blue-white lightning over West Mountain and it was
getting dark. But not too dark for Leo to aim Grandfather's
pistol at the deserted bottled-in-bond fifth or quart or whatever it was and squeeze the trigger again after squinting one
eye shut. At a range of about three feet, he hit what he was
aiming at and the bottle exploded in a shower of shards and
amber liquid.

Then Leo turned and walked back off the platform and to
the corner of the station where the debris of the broken barrel lay scattered about, and threw down his stave with all the
rest of the dismembered water receptacle and said, "They
sure'n hell ruint a good rain barrel."

By the time Leo Sparks got back to Grandfather's house,
he was soaking wet, but I don't imagine he gave a damn. He'd
had his victory over the Castleberry bunch and even over the
memory of their goddamned Airedale besides. When he
handed the pistol to Grandfather, he said, "I'll pay you for
the bullets I used."

Well, it turned out that it was more than Leo's victory. It
belonged to the whole town. Because to the best of anybody's knowledge, that July evening was the last time Arlis
Castleberry or Monet Scrub ever appeared on the streets of
Weedy Rough. Within a week they were established in a hotel at the county seat, finishing all the business it required to
get the hell out of Arkansas and down to Texas.

The wounded Ford roadster remained in the yard behind

the brick house, one tire flat and the radiator punctured, until it was hauled off to be repaired by the man who bought the property, a guy from Kansas City who owned a string of moving-picture-show theaters through southern Missouri.

It may have made everybody else in the Rough happy, but I was disappointed as hell. At least for a while, until I grew up. Being bloodthirsty, like most kids are at a tender age, I'd wanted a gun in the house that had killed somebody. But all I got was a little pistol that had wounded a yellow car.

So the years went down and the story grew and then after a while died, when those who had seen it or heard the shots from the depot platform that night faded away and were buried. And it cropped up again after that, until finally it was said that Leo Sparks had wounded Monet Scrub in the foot, and then in the leg, and, before it had run its course, that he had killed somebody.

Leo Sparks didn't kill anything. Except those dogs who happened to eat his poisoned chicken bones.

There was a lot more. The last time I talked to Esta Stayborn before he died, around the time of General Eisenhower's first heart attack, he told me some things.

"That brick house had been willed to Monet Scrub," Esta said.

"Damn, I didn't realize Big Cooney put that much store in the son of a bitch," I said.

"I didn't either," said Esta. "But I talked to Old Doc Jones before he shot himself. He was a witness to the will. Monet Scrub was Big Cooney's son."

It made a lot of sense to anybody who had ever known Big Cooney Castleberry that he'd bring a mistress right under his own roof for afternoon hardball. And then be so arrogantly proud of his progeny as to announce it in a legal document.

"You think Monet knew it?" I asked.

"Beans on the table, beans in the mouth," Esta said. "That was Monet."

"You think Mrs. Lillian knew it?"

"Mrs. Lillian was not a very aggressive person," Esta said. "And she wasn't stupid, either."

So that was something to think about down through the years, Mrs. Lillian sitting there in her nice brick house parlor, doing needlepoint and knowing that in the back of the house something besides needlepoint was happening.

And when the result of this in-house philandering issued, right there under her very own roof, her taking the baby and giving it every affection and advantage she tried to give her own, knowing as she did that the squalling brat was the final, absolute token of Big Cooney Castleberry's infidelity, and seeing the years advance and understanding that this son who was alien to her own body was an abomination to the same extent that her own blood son was, perhaps thinking all along, hoping all along, that at least one of the two would be something she could remember with pride on the last day she spent before going to the grave in Fort Smith.

It was something to think about down through the years.

For the rest of it, the Scrub family bought a used Dodge truck, with some of the money Lula got for her son from Big Cooney, I suspect, and drove off to California at the height of the dust storms that blew in over the hills from the plains, making everything smell like a slide into second base after a month of no rain. Nobody ever heard from any of them again.

Arlis, so Esta Stayborn told me, made a fortune on brown grocery bags he'd hoarded, a couple of boxcar loads, before the war broke out and such things became almost extinct. Of course, he didn't need to make any fortune because his daddy had left him plenty, and nobody was willing to guess how he was smart enough to know that brown grocery bags would become as precious as gold at about the same time the federal government started issuing ration stamps that were necessary to buy a piece of beefsteak in the meat market.

Monet went to the Texas state penitentiary in Huntsville for a long stay on a conviction for arson. Like Esta Stayborn said, Monet always liked to watch fires.

And Leo?

Well, like I've said, he lived a long time, sitting on his front porch after all the rest of his family was gone. Likely thinking about the July evening he made up for all that Airedale dogshit in his yard.

Somebody, about a week after they buried him at Bethel Ford, put a little sandstone rock at the head of his still-fresh grave. Just a rock. There was no inscription on it. It was just a rock, like a few at other graves over people who had been put down as far back as the Civil War. And when I looked at it, I knew that within a few years the pale green moss would begin to grow up over it and nobody would have the slightest notion about whom it represented.

Well, as long as I've got left, one person will know. I'll know. Even though I'm still a little put out that on the evening of the July rain on the depot platform in Weedy Rough, Leo Sparks shot a Ford instead of Arlis Castleberry.

3

Once a Year

Before Shanks Caulder ever
came to the county seat and civilization, he had known fox
racing. He knew it as it can only be known by one who has
been around a wooded hillside fire after the stars are out, and
listened to the dogs running, their clear and vibrant voices
like no other sound in this or any other world.

There was a spiritual quality to it, as though the night sky
were the diamond-sprinkled dome of a great cathedral where
only the most reverent had gathered. And this regardless of
the patched overalls and the fractured grammar that were
standard in the circle of orange light around the blazing oak
logs.

Everyone who ever experienced it, that sound of foxhounds running in the deep night, became a philosopher. But
few ever expressed in words what they had known. Perhaps
they were incapable of expressing it, or reckoned it something to which only they were privy and nobody else would
understand it anyway. Or more likely they felt that it was a
sacred realm, like posted property, where strangers were ac-
tively discouraged from entering.

Mostly, they have gone to their graves in silence, never ex-

*plaining the light that used to come into their eyes in sum-
mer when the sun was going down and there was the prospect
of somebody, somewhere, releasing a pack of hounds onto the
fox population.*

*But Shanks can never keep his mouth shut. About any-
thing. And certainly not about those times around the night
fires, listening to the men talk and the dogs run. He was just
a kid then, generally unnoticed except by his grandfather, and
would nibble the canned corned beef, which they called tin
willy, and chew on hunks of the rubbery yellow cheese, perhaps even taking a sip now and again from one of the mason
jars containing the white lightning, when his grandfather
wasn't looking. Slowly he learned to hear, and to realize that
there were notes of anguish and despair and joy and jubila-
tion filtering through the stands of white oak and hickory
timber, the voices of the dogs sending their message straight
up past the North Star and the Big Dipper and the Milky
Way, sending their music of life and death past everything,
to eternity.*

*Well, it's been a long time since they've had that kind of
fox race in the hills. But Shanks remembers, and he speaks
of it now and again, still amazed and always trying to relate
it somehow to things human.*

And why not? Shanks has heard the music.

We're talking foxhounds here. And not the kind that goes out in the afternoon sun and always followed by a bunch of people in red coats and beanie hats and some guy with a little trumpet, and after the fox is caught everybody goes back to the castle and has a few jolts of what these folks call whiskey but is really Scotch and then they go into the dining room for kidney pie or some such thing, all the while talking about what a good run the little red-tailed bounder made before the dogs caught him and mauled him to death, and while they're eating, some jocko behind the stables is skinning out what's left of the fox so that maybe Lady Bottomwell can have a nice fur piece for her fall coat.

Hell, we're talking fox *races* here. Where nobody wants to catch the fox, maybe least of all the dogs, who just might understand that when the fox is caught he won't be around for another run tomorrow night. And a race held *only* at night. And the hunters aren't really hunters at all, but talkers and listeners who stand around a fire, warming their butts and chewing tobacco, rough-cut plug, and eating tin willy Grandfather or Esta Stayborn has brought out from town, and a few taking a long swig of clear corn from a fruit jar during moments of lull in the action out in the woods.

And each one of these old guys can tell you exactly which dog is leading the pack, even though at that moment the pack may be more than a mile away and in some deep hollow so you have to strain to even hear their voices. Then they come up over a ridge and the sound is so clear and hard it's like they just jumped out of your hip pocket and they're still almost a mile away.

Resonance and timbre. Fire and fury. That's what they sound like, a good pack running. Like Mozart and Wagner rolled into one. And I know a little bit about guys like Mozart and Wagner because I played some of their stuff on the trombone and I listened to a helluva lot more of it on records.

And you know that out there in the darkness the fox is running before the dogs without a sound. And he knows he can have all the fun he wants and when he gets tired of it he can lose the pack in two minutes flat. He'll den or tree, and the dogs go crazy because they know they've lost him.

Unless it's right after a big rain and the ground and the timber and underbrush is wet. Then the fox is in deep trouble, because the scent is strong and the hounds come on fast. Only stupid foxes go out to challenge the dogs after a big rain.

You didn't know a fox could tree? They can. And usually

they'll sit in some persimmon bush while the dogs rush under them and on into a confused mob and then the tone of their voices is different. It says, "We've lost the little son of a bitch." And while the pack is thrashing around, the fox slides down from his persimmon tree and goes off to do fox things, like maybe he trots back to the den where the vixen and the kits have been listening, and you can almost see him smiling, trotting through the dark timber.

So that's when the guys around the fire spit and cuss and say "Dadgummit, I guess they lost him," which means the race is finished for the night. So dadgummit, take out the hill-country trumpet, which is a whittled cow's horn, and blow in the dogs, though you know damned well you can blow that horn until you're blue in the face and the dogs won't pay any attention to it and will wander around in the woods the rest of the night looking for the fox and will finally come in home when they're damned good and ready.

Then the guys get on their mules or their bay mares or climb into their tin lizzies and head off home, and the final one there takes the last of the corn whiskey and stomps out the fire and then lights his lantern and starts to walk home because somehow it always seems to work out that this last guy doesn't have a mule or a bay mare or a tin lizzy. Maybe that's why the other guys always leave him a few swigs of the corn to help him along on his journey through the night.

Sometimes a few of those dogs would stay out for two or three days before they came dragging in home, hungry and scratched and loaded with burrs. But after a day or so of hog cracklings and table slops, they were ready to go again.

Maybe that's why hill men loved foxhounds. Because no matter how many times they went out and ran and lost, not having caught the fox, once they'd had a little breather and some chow, they were anxious to go again. You couldn't defeat those fox dogs, like you can a lot of people.

In the woods at night, listening to them running, you had

this feeling that it was all one living thing, the whole pack. Like a tiger with many voices. But when they came dragging in home a day or so later, then you saw the individuals.

Like Trixie.

I could look at Trixie and see travel to far and strange places. And maybe a little mystery that mere humans couldn't even see was there, much less define.

This is just a foxhound, you understand, and when I knew her, a pretty old one. Just a damned old dog. Not very big except for her eyes and mouth. She had these splashes of color on a dirty white fur coat. Splashes of brown and bay and black in no particular order. In fact, sometimes I swore the pattern of colors changed just because old Trixie had gotten tired of the former arrangement. She had a tongue and a tail of about equal lengths, at either end of her lank body above those long running legs. She wasn't any beauty. Until you'd heard her run.

Trixie smelled pretty bad when you got close enough to scratch her ears. I always had the feeling she didn't give a good damn whether you got close enough to scratch her ears or not. It was like she knew there were other qualities that outranked ear-scratching and odor.

It was like she knew all of that was just surface stuff that any outland city guy would remark on, but for her friends, like me and Grandfather, she knew the only thing that mattered was the voice and those long running legs. And maybe she didn't give a damn about that either, about having friends like me and Grandfather. He told me once that Trixie or any other good fox dog could live in the woods alone if they wanted to, catching squirrels and rabbits and birds to eat, and maybe the only reason they allowed themselves to be penned and fed by some human man was just for a few laughs while they watched these people taking baths and wearing clothes and that kind of shit.

But anyway, what she really counted for was the music she

made in the woods when she was hot in after a gray fox. Or a red, for that matter. And when you heard her run, you knew she was right. That was when she became something other than flesh and bone, just a voice in the night, like a ghost, haunting all those hills and hollows and deserted fallow fields and burned-out rock farms where nothing was left but the blackened sandstone chimney and the bluffs and creeks and the shades of old Osage Indians who had come to those hills for a little orangewood to make bows. She'd be headlong after the fox, singing her tune, and it was some tune, by God.

And it was like she knew you'd never figure all that out, all the stuff that went through her head. All the notes she made with her voice. Trixie became, for me, when I was just a dumb kid, the whole kit and kaboodle of fox dogs, all the runners of the hillsides rolled into one twenty-five-pound package of exploding energy in the race and of haughty indolence in the dooryard.

She was one helluva hound. But she never let anybody get to know her too well. That's what real fox dogs are all about.

You don't see many real fox dogs anymore. You see a lot of beagles and a few bassets and other breeds I can't even name, all called hounds but not one of them that knows anything about how to sing a tune in the night that makes goose bumps jump out on your arms.

Back in the hills, there used to be people who were just like fox dogs. They didn't run through the woods chasing varmints, of course, but they had the same mystery about them. Like you couldn't reach them, no matter how you tried. And like old Trixie, they wouldn't tell you. Maybe like Trixie, they couldn't. Even if they'd wanted to, which I doubt they did.

So when I was a kid, I could look at one of those hounds and wonder where it'd been, what it'd seen and felt, out there in the wilderness. And now that I'm a grown man, it's worse. Because now I don't just wonder where that dog might have been. I worry about *what* that dog might have been.

It all started during those hazy, dust-smelling afternoons when I sat on the back porch of Grandfather's house in Weedy Rough and Grandfather would have one of his dogs between his legs, picking the ticks off its ears and scratching its back and telling me how Old Ted or Old Casper or Old Macy sounded when they hit a fresh fox trail.

"After a long time of listening," Grandfather would say, "maybe thirty years, you can tell from the sound of them whether it's a red fox or a gray. And pretty soon you know, because the reds will den out on you quick. But the grays will run half the night."

God, the very thought, even now, of being out there around a fire somewhere and Grandfather telling me about what dog's doing what while we listen, it makes a hard knot in the chest. And Grandfather dead now for thirty years. Died, in fact, the same year that Trixie got caught trying to cross a paved highway and was run over by a car. By some drunk, likely, who never knew he'd snuffed out a thing that meant more than him and all his progeny would ever mean because none of them could make the cold chills go up your back.

Grandfather used to say the dogs would run clear over into Oklahoma, if the fox was so inclined. Clear over into the Cookson Hills. Pretty Boy Floyd country. And back then, the Cookson Hills were as far away as China. That was before they put concrete on all those hill roads and brought Weedy Rough into the modern world, before they paved the federal highway just on the other side of East Mountain. One of the first things that happened after they laid down the hard slab along that route was when Trixie got caught on it and run over and killed. Grandfather always hated that road, ever after.

It's still there. Only now there aren't any fox dogs to kill. Just people, on that road.

Anyway, Grandfather would be scratching a hound's ear and he'd look across the valley toward West Mountain and he'd get this faraway glaze in his eyes. It was those times I started comparing some hill folk we knew to Trixie and the other dogs. Because Grandfather always did.

"Old Man Shearson," he said one day. "Now, there'd be a good runner after the fox, except I don't think his voice would carry too far through the woods."

Then Grandfather would laugh that little chuckle of his that sounded like it was meant only for himself alone. And I'd think about Old Man Shearson.

Once each year Old Man Shearson came out of the hills around Devil's Mountain. That was before they had a lake and a big recreational area there. He rode a gray mule that was old enough to have belonged to Belle Starr and he carried a rifle, and behind him on the mule's rump was a shaggy bundle of hides he had trapped. He would appear on West Mountain early in the morning, meaning he had ridden all night from his shack or cave or whatever it was he lived in, wherever it was, back in the wild border country next to Oklahoma. He would come down the West Mountain road, hunched over, with the rifle across his thighs, looking straight ahead and never slipping one way or the other no matter how crookedly the mule walked, even though he was riding bareback.

The few people who were awake that early got out of his way as he came into the street by the blacksmith shop. He rode with a straightforward purpose, or maybe it was resignation, past the bank and around the corner to Esta Stayborn's general mercantile store. There he would rein in and sit for a while, seeming too stiff to dismount, and then finally slide off the mule and pull his hides with him.

He would cross the wood plank sidewalk and stoop, being well over six feet tall, to peer through the dirty glass door until he was sure no one was about yet. Then he would drop his hides on the sidewalk and his rifle on top of them and squat, leaning against the building and looking straight out into the street.

Sometimes a dog would wander along in front of the buildings of Weedy Rough's west side, stop a few minutes and stare at the old man and then, maybe getting a whiff of his aroma, turn and trot on across the railroad tracks and stand at the depot scratching and looking back to be sure that the old man wasn't following him.

About eight o'clock, Esta Stayborn would come down off the hill where he had his house and pull a big ring of keys from his pocket to open the door. He'd see the old man, but neither of them would speak and in fact Old Man Shearson would act as though Esta Stayborn wasn't even there.

When he got inside, Esta always checked over his store receipts for the past week, trying to figure out how much he could afford to pay for a bundle of worthless hides. No matter how he figured it, he knew that when the old man came in, he'd lose some money. But he also knew that he'd always buy the hides.

After maybe an hour or so, Old Man Shearson would rise from his squat and take the hides and the rifle inside. He threw them on the counter, those smelly pelts, each year the same way, without looking at Esta or much of anything else. And the rifle would lie there on the hides like some sort of token and Esta knew it wasn't for sale so he'd take the rifle and put it aside and unwrap the bundle of hides and finger them and make little sounds that were supposed to mean something or other, then go to his cash drawer and take out the few bills he could afford to pay the old man.

And with Esta watching him, the old man would say, "I need some overhalls." Or maybe it was a hat.

Esta sold him what he needed, at wholesale prices although he never told the old man that, and watched the old man pick up his overalls or hat or whatever and the rifle and walk out and Esta knew he wouldn't be back for a year.

Somehow, Old Man Shearson never trusted Esta Stayborn's ammunition, so after he untied his mule he'd walk across the tracks to Shirvy's store and get a box of .38-40s for the old Marlin rifle. Then he'd go up the hill behind the bank to Violet Sims's house, the mule following along like a dog with his head down, and inside Old Man Shearson always laid whatever money he had left on Violet's kitchen table and she'd open the top of her footstool and take out a bootleg bottle from the supply there. It was usually a fifth of clear corn or sometimes only a pint. It all depended on how much profit Esta Stayborn had made over the past week.

It never changed, year after year, and by nine o'clock Old Man Shearson could be seen in the tie yard, sitting with his back against a stack of posts or stays or crossties, the fruit jar of corn in his hand, and he'd stay there sipping until all the coal-oil-scented whiskey was gone, then throw the empty fruit jar onto the tracks, get on the mule, and ride past the bank, around the corner toward the blacksmith shop, and up West Mountain.

Nobody bothered him. Nobody said anything to him. Everybody stayed as far away from him as they could because he smelled so bad and he looked so mean. Nobody knew anything about him. No one had ever seen where he lived. No one cared. He'd just come into town, sell his hides, make his necessary purchases, and sit in the center of Weedy Rough and drink his corn liquor and Prohibition be damned and nobody bothered him.

I used to sit in Grandmother's west window and look down into the tie yard and watch Old Man Shearson drink. God, I can still hear the flies and smell the dust and feel the constriction in my throat just like I did when I was a kid, seeing him lift that fruit jar to his mouth, and me so young I didn't even know what corn whiskey tasted like but I knew it was a hellish sin.

Old Man Shearson lived out in those hills alone for a long time. Then, right after the Great War, he got a wife. Anyway, people said it was right after the Great War, but they weren't sure. Nobody knew how long he'd had her.

Little bits and pieces were put together from the stories of squirrel hunters and timber cutters. She was an Indian, they all said. And the story went that the old man got tired of being alone so he went over into Oklahoma and got a woman, a Cherokee or maybe a Creek. Sometimes they'd be seen together, back in the deep woods, him with his rifle and riding that mule and her walking along behind, wearing a calico Montgomery Ward dress that she must have brought with her to her bridal bed because sure as hell Old Man Shearson had never bought anything like that in Esta Stayborn's store.

So far as history records, nobody in Weedy Rough ever saw this woman. She never came in when the old man did. But she was out there, all right. Later, there was proof of that.

The old man kept coming once a year, getting older than the rocks but staying pretty much the same. He was big, not fat big but bone big, like the bluetick hound you could use for hunting bear. His hands were long and scaly, with blue veins running across them. His face was flat and hard and looked like leather on an old saddle, but his eyes were pale, sharp, and clear. He didn't seem to blink much. Esta Stayborn, who always saw him closer than anybody else, said the old man had wolf eyes, yellow and brittle as the best glassie in a kid's marble sack.

I guess every small town had to have somebody it could threaten its kids with, and in Weedy Rough that somebody was Old Man Shearson. Having seen him at a distance or not at all, the women of the town held him out to their youngsters as the world's very worst wicked evil who would creep up in the night and snatch them away to the woods if they insisted on making a lot of racket over going to bed so early. So the kids went silently to bed, in the dark, hearing every groan of hickory limb against the eaves, every creak of old floor joists settling, every whisper of loose screen against the window, and knowing in their hearts that those sounds were really the hands searching for them. Until finally the kids were petrified, not sleeping really, just lying there waiting like the guy on death row, waiting for the hands to find them. And in Weedy Rough, the hands belonged to Old Man Shearson.

When I was young and tender, I was afraid of almost everything. But somehow nobody ever bothered to threaten me with that old man, even knowing as they must have that only threats would make me hush when it was time for bed. Maybe because Grandmother knew he wasn't a thing that would frighten me, for she had some inkling, like grandmothers have about such things, some inkling that there was a relationship between me and Old Man Shearson sealed in the dust smell of her front room when he was in that tie yard and I was safely behind her windowpane. And knowing that whatever it was, or whatever sealed it, I just simply wasn't afraid of him.

We got to be friends, me and that old man, although he never knew it. Me in the safety of Grandmother's living room and him down there in the Frisco tie yard. He looked like an old rag bag, with knots of brown wrist and ankle bone peeking out at different places. He would sit there with his sweat-stained hatbrim shading his wolf eyes and lift the fruit jar to his mouth and I could almost see the lumpy Adam's apple jerking up and down.

He was just like a very old foxhound, and in those days when I shared his corn liquor with him, I wondered where he'd run, in the night, alone. Just like I wondered about Trixie when I watched Grandfather scratching her ears. It was all the same. A little bit of fear and a little bit of respect, which is sometimes the same thing.

Well, on one trip into town, Old Man Shearson brought a baby with him. A nut-brown little baby boy, wrapped in a dirty blanket and peering out from the smelly folds with large black eyes, never whimpering or making any sound even though it was obvious he needed a change of clothes, maybe three or four times over.

At first, Esta Stayborn thought the old man wanted to sell

the baby along with his hides, but finally Old Man Shearson made Esta understand that he only wanted to leave the baby for somebody else to take care of, because the backwoods wasn't too good a place to have a baby getting in the way of hunting and trapping and doing all the other things that a man had to do in the back woods.

Esta yelled about it and said he couldn't take care of it and Old Man Shearson said Esta could sure as hell find somebody who could and Esta yelled it was all against the law and Old Man Shearson said the law could go jump in the gawddamned lake.

The discussion ended when the old man walked out, got on his mule, and rode up West Mountain without even bothering to get any money for his hides or buy any rifle ammunition or even any whiskey, and Esta Stayborn knew he wouldn't see the old man for another year. But it was longer than that. Nobody in Weedy Rough ever saw the old man again.

Anyway, Esta bent over the bundle lying there on his counter and he could smell the woodsmoke and grease and a lot of other things and he looked at the baby and the baby looked back without batting an eye.

"Oh, Lord," Esta said, and called the sheriff.

It wasn't long after that when one of the woodcutters came in saying he'd seen the old man's squaw, or rather her body, because she was dead. It looked like smallpox or some such thing had got her, and she had been dead awhile when the woodcutter came across her body. They buried what was left of her, the woodcutter said, and he doubted he could find the grave out there in the tie-oaks and the sheriff said it didn't make much difference because she was just an Indian anyway and had never voted in the Democratic primary and in fact had never been in Weedy Rough or anywhere else in the county that he knew of, except maybe out there in the woods. As far as anyone could swear to, she had never lived. He said it was best just to leave it at that.

Of course, she'd lived, all right. There was that baby.

Esta Stayborn kept it a few days and then the sheriff found a middle-aged couple in Brentwoolsy who didn't have any kids of their own and were happy to take the baby.

Old Man Shearson bringing a live baby into town created a real stir. Not as much as when the town caught fire, which it did on a periodic basis, but a considerable stir just the same. Esta Stayborn became the center of attention until every last drop of juice was squeezed out of him about what-all had happened.

When Esta unwrapped that bundle, there was even more mess than the odor had suggested. Esta took the baby, buck naked, out behind his store and dipped it into the creek there and got it cleaned off. That water was cold but the baby didn't make any racket about it.

"I dunked him in there a few times," Esta said. "But all he done was blink."

Inside the blanket was a large piece of brown sack paper, and scrawled across it were the words *John Wesley Shearson*.

Esta Stayborn thought about that name for a long time, and later, after the child had already been taken in adoption by the couple in Brentwoolsy, he was lying beside his wife in bed one night and said into the darkness, maybe not even talking to anyone but himself, "Where the hell did he get that name? I never reckoned him much of a church person."

In fact, Old Man Shearson was no church person at all. He hadn't named his son after the great Methodist. But nobody knew that at the time, and the women in the Ladies' Aid Society said maybe the kid had a chance in life after all, even being born like he was to a dirty old woods hunter and some Indian squaw, because he had a handle that gave him a head start on Christian sobriety and cleanliness and purity. How could you go wrong with a name like that, they said.

It wasn't until years later, after most of those same women of the Ladies' Aid Society had long since gone to their re-

ward, that somebody who made a lifework of poking around
in dusty archives and reading old newspapers and diaries
came up with the real source of the name, and by that time
nobody gave a damn one way or the other. Not even John
Wesley Shearson himself, because by then he had grown to
manhood and enlisted in the United States Marine Corps and
won the Navy Cross for valor at a place called Iwo Jima and
got killed in the process.

Old Man Shearson must have been at least eighty when his
son was born. He covered a long span, even though nobody
who knew him in Weedy Rough ever thought about him as
ever having been young. But there had been times when he'd
seen cattle going up to the railroads in Kansas, across the
dusty prairies of the Indian Nations. And he'd spent a lot of
nights beside trail fires along the Red and the Cimarron and
the Verdigris rivers.

Once, in the Texas hill country, he'd been involved in a
card game at one of those little crossroads shacks where
drovers and whiskey merchants and Mexicans and a few men
who would not admit occupation or origin gathered in the
evening to eat cheese and drink warm beer and brag about the
women they had known in San Antonio. There were six people in this card game. History does not record what game it
might have been, but chances are great that it was five-card
stud.

Somebody, in the course of determining the winner of a pot,
dropped a queen of clubs from a loose sleeve and all hell
broke loose. When the racket and the black-powder smoke
had cleared a little, two men walked out. One was Old Man
Shearson. Only he wasn't old then. The other was a gentle-
man between stints as a guest in various Texas jails and the
big pen at Huntsville, and it was just a short while before he
was shot dead in an El Paso saloon. His name was John
Wesley Hardin.

Well, previous to any of this being known, somebody with

a sense of humor named a little town Shearson. It's still there, in the hills south of Weedy Rough, just a couple of buildings, and the road that runs through it toward Devil's Mountain from the federal highway is barely wide enough for a single log wagon. The railroad passes right through it. But the train never stops there.

4

The Saga of Slaven Budd

He's never put it into words,
but to Shanks Caulder, historical perspective has nothing to
do with presidents or political parties or wars or the stability
of the economy or revolutions like the Industrial and the
Technological. Historical perspective, to Shanks, is a gut
feeling. An ambiance. He maintains that any town is made
up of three equal parts, the whole of which defines its character: hence, historical perspective.

First, there's the physical plant, a term he picked up in the
army. This includes the terrain and the buildings and the
roads and the railroads and all the other actual objects anyone can see or touch.

Second is the flavor of the era, and nobody knows where
Shanks picked up that term. To him it means how a town
smells and how the food that comes from its tables tastes.
How the pulse of life sounds there, the beating of the community heart, so to speak.

And finally, the people.

Shanks Caulder concentrates on the people in his stories—
which is natural, considering that he is one of them. And
when he tells about life after he came to the county seat, one

always has the feeling that he is talking about normal, rational, ordinary people.

But when he goes back to Weedy Rough in his memory, there is an odd gleam in his eye and a barely suppressed astonishment in his voice that somehow conveys that this earlier period was very strange yet glorious to him. Stories from that time are like a recitation of mystic chords, unheard by civilized ears, like a canvas of colors unknown to sophisticated eyes. And sometimes there's a poison vapor that wrinkles the nose.

You get the feeling that Weedy Rough and its people left a lot of scar tissue on the hide and soul of Shanks Caulder. And that he treasures each hurt.

The Budd family was the wonder and despair of Weedy Rough.

There was the patriarch, Harmon. He'd lost a leg under the wheels of a rolling Frisco freight train when he worked for the railroad, and had refused their offer of a fine cork limb. He cut his own peg leg from a hickory sapling and strapped it on with a couple of old leather belts.

At least the Frisco paid him a small pension for the rest of his life.

Harmon's greatest claim to fame was one he never under-

stood. It was said that he'd actually seen, in the flesh and with
all their automatic rifles beside them, Bonnie Parker and
Clyde Barrow when the romantic pair, if that's the right word
for them, stopped at Cobb Hub's filling station on the federal
highway. Harmon happened to be sitting there among the
bottles of engine oil and cases of Nehi soda pop, having a few
afternoon sips of elderberry wine from a quart mason jar.
When the Model B Ford pulled up and Clyde Barrow got out
and made known his need for five gallons of gas and a few
decks of Camel cigarettes, Harmon Budd looked at him and
thought he was probably an enforcement officer for the Volstead Act and so hid his mason jar of elderberry wine under
the bib of his overalls and left it there until the Ford pulled
off in a cloud of limestone gravel dust and a puff of blue ex-
haust smoke.

Later, when the people in Weedy Rough asked about him
seeing these two famous people, Harmon Budd blinked and
licked his lips and hitched up the belts that held his hickory-
sapling peg leg in place and said, "Who the hell is Bonnie
Parker and Clyde Barrow? They live around here some-
wheres?"

Anyway, the railroad pension kept Harmon Budd in booze
for about the first two weeks of each month. After that, nobody knew where he got money enough to be drunk each
night, decorating the north end of the Frisco depot when the
train came through, sprawled against a big maple tree, his peg
leg thrust out before him and the dogs coming up to sniff his
one good foot, which was housed in a broken brogan, while
people in the passenger coaches looked out and pointed at him
and said, "Look at that quaint man."

And nobody could figure out how he fed his kids. There
were plenty of them. There was Slaven, the oldest boy, and
then Hominy and Little Sue and Chink and Violet Rose and
Frisco and Red Gum and Number One, who was named after
the high bridge just south of the Weedy Rough railroad tun-

nel. Everybody called that first trestle Number One because there were two more bridges farther down the valley. They were Number Two and Number Three.

Nobody ever saw much of Harmon's wife, Big Sue. She wasn't really very big but she had been called that to distinguish her from her third born ever since Little Sue had arrived. Big Sue had pale green eyes, which she gave to all her kids, and those who did see her when she ventured from the Budd shack that was in the woods behind the blacksmith shop said her hair was mouse-colored and looked like maybe it hadn't been combed since the Armistice. She was mostly hide and bone with a lot of sharp angles around the shoulders and hips that loose gingham dresses couldn't completely conceal.

Big Sue and taken her fair share of licks from Harmon Budd's peg leg on those occasions when he came home drunk and took it off to use as a club to maintain order in his household. Everybody said if she acted a little crazy it was no great surprise, what with the way Harmon treated her.

Some of the rougher element in town enjoyed teasing Harmon about his wife's family. She'd been a Magurk, one of those wild hill families that lived far out in the sticks and were about as inbred as a pack of foxhounds. The fun-and-frolic boys would come up to Harmon when he was lying drunk beside the depot and taunt him with the fact that Big Sue's brothers were always hanging around his shack when he was gone. Harmon would charge about on his peg leg, making all kinds of vile threats.

The teasing about Big Sue's brothers wasn't as bad as the peg-leg hide-and-go-seek the town toughs played. They'd slip Harmon's leg off when he was asleep and then stand around in front of the drugstore across the street from the depot and wait for him to wake up. When that happened, Harmon would discover his leg was missing and he'd roar and crawl around in the dust of the street, slobbering and cussing.

This would go on until one of Harmon's kids appeared. It

was usually Slaven, because Harmon's eldest son seemed to feel some responsibility toward his daddy and tried to keep an eye on him now and then. Slaven would retrieve the leg from its hiding place in the culvert under Joe Sanford's ice cream parlor. Holding the leg like a baseball bat, Slaven would approach his old man with great caution. About ten feet short of the still-bellowing Harmon, Slaven would throw the leg in his daddy's general direction and then run like hell, because he knew that once Harmon got his hands on that hickory stick he'd whale anybody within range.

Slaven Budd was my age almost to the day. He wasn't a bad-looking kid, but there was always something strange about him, like maybe he was listening to a lot of sounds nobody else could hear. Part of it may have been those pale green eyes or the way he carried himself, looking as though one of his skinny arms was about to fly off in its own independent direction. Or maybe it was because he never found much to talk about and when a sound did issue from his thin lips it was usually just a grunt or else a string of words run together so fast people couldn't figure out what the hell he was talking about.

Slaven had had his fair share of whacks from that peg leg, too. But that had been in his younger days, before he'd learned how to dodge and otherwise avoid his daddy. Sometimes he'd sleep in the woods rather than go home, when Harmon was in a particularly ugly mood.

I always figured the kid had a lot of talent. He was quicker on his feet than Violet Sims's cat, and would have made a great shortstop, but he never joined in games with the other guys because so many of them were always teasing him about his mother or his daddy. And besides, they never asked him to join in. He'd stand around and watch whatever it was the other kids were doing and after a while pick up a rock and throw it like a shot and it'd hit an oak tree fifty yards away with a smack like slapping a barrel stave against the side of a barn. Then he'd just walk off into the woods, all alone, stopping every few steps to pick up another rock and throw it with a whip of his skinny right arm, whack against another oak tree.

Well, he wasn't completely alone. There were the dogs. It was amazing, but every yard dog in town loved Slaven Budd. He could make a few guttural sounds and dogs would come down off the surrounding hills and swarm around him with their tails about to twist off their butts and their tongues out like they were laughing, and Slaven would make a few more grunts and wheezes and coughs and those dogs would go crazy with delight. Slaven may not have been much for human talking, but he sure as hell could speak dog.

During berry time, early risers could see Slaven and the rest of the Budd kids trooping out into the woods to pick wild huckleberries. They took along these little half-gallon syrup pails with wire bails. It took a long time to fill one of those buckets with the little hill variety of wild berry, but back in Weedy Rough they could get a dime for each bucketful. Slaven wasn't much of a berry picker. He'd get out there in the heavy timber and forget what he was there for and start smelling wild flowers and digging grubs out of old rotten logs. He always took along a few dozen town dogs for company.

Sometimes Slaven would become so intent in his study of nature that the sun would go down and it would get dark and he'd still be three miles out of town in the wilderness. He didn't give a damn. He'd just bed down in the leaves with the dogs all around him, packed tight against him like a breathing blanket. Slaven smelled pretty doggy.

He went to school, but nobody really knew why. They seated him in the fourth grade and just left him there. Each new class that came in had to get used to his occasional outbursts of dog language right in the middle of Miss Laveta's oration on the Missouri-Mississippi river system. Eventually the other kids came to ignore him and education made its

inexorable march right past Slaven Budd until finally, when
he was as big as Miss Laveta, he just stopped coming.

"They ain't got nothin' in that school but horseshit," he
said to me. It was true, I could understand him when he
spoke. Me and the dogs.

It was funny, but nobody ever picked a fight with him. And
some of those hill kids didn't figure the day was complete
without getting into at least one good contest of fists, as I
found out. Slaven would have been glad to oblige. He was a
brave kid. Many's the time in the street beside the Frisco depot he'd wade into a dogfight and pull the antagonists apart,
no matter the flashing teeth.

And everybody knew that the few times Slaven got care-
less and came too close to his old man and Harmon belted
him with that peg leg, Slaven would just blink those pale green
eyes and shrug his skinny shoulders and walk away, usually
saying the only three words anybody ever heard him speak
to his daddy: "You dirty bastard!"

About once each year, the Methodist Church Ladies' Aid
Society tried to do something for the Budd family. One year
they collected a basket of groceries and took it down to the
depot and placed it beside Harmon, who was sitting against
his own personal maple tree, a little over two-thirds drunk.
Harmon thanked the ladies for himself and for his wife and
for his children and said the Lord God would bless them all
for their Christian charity. Then, as soon as the ladies had
trooped back up the hill toward the Methodist parsonage,
where they would sip lemonade and nibble ginger snaps and
talk about how maybe there was hope for the Budd family if
they just continued their good work, Harmon took the basket
of groceries over behind Esta Stayborn's general mercantile
store and ate it all himself.

Harmon got sick as hell and puked in the little stream there
behind Esta's store, and Esta said it likely killed all the fish
for seven miles down the West Fork of White River.

When the Ladies' Aid Society or the Eastern Star had a pie sale under the shed at the south end of the Frisco depot, anything they had left over they gave to the Budd kids. That didn't work much better than the basket of groceries they'd given to Harmon, because Slaven, being the oldest and biggest, would take everything away from the other kids and run off into the woods with it, where he and his dog friends would have a little feast. It was amazing how many house dogs around Weedy Rough developed a taste for lemon pie.

No account of Slaven Budd would be complete without a mention of Claude Gones. Claude was about sixty years old the first time the people of Weedy Rough got to know him. He stayed about sixty for the next twenty years. He just appeared one day out of the hills, all tattered and ragged and with a lisp and two old brown eyes and a perpetual growth of beard. The beard was a mystery because it never got any longer over the years, although everybody knew that Claude had not touched hand to razor in all that time, and certainly no such thing as shaving soap, or soap in any form, had ever touched his cheeks.

He lived mostly on ice cream cones he bought at Joe Sanford's ice cream parlor with dimes that he got from various citizens and fox hunters in the town, and a little bait of baloney and cheese he begged at Violet Sims's back door. There were some who maintained that now and then Violet Sims took Claude into her bed, without her usual demand for payment, just for the pure hell of it. Nobody ever proved it.

Anyway, sometimes Claude and Slaven Budd got into one helluva fistfight on the sidewalk outside the ice cream parlor or maybe the drugstore after Claude had done his usual routine. "You got a dime, Mr. Stayborn?"—or Mr. Pay or Mr. Merton or anybody that Claude thought might have ten cents in his pocket, and then he'd go into the ice cream parlor or the drugstore and buy an ice cream cone. Always strawberry. And sometimes, no sooner would Claude come back out onto the street with his ice cream cone to observe the passing scene than Slaven Budd would confront him with the proposition that maybe Claude ought to do the Christian thing and allow Slaven to have a few licks of that strawberry.

Then the fight would start, because in the memory of all citizens of Weedy Rough, Claude never once agreed to let Slaven Budd have a lick of his ice cream cone.

Olie Merton called it the Great Ice Cream War, and it broke out every summer with monotonous regularity.

Slaven always won, of course. He weighed about eighty pounds more than the old man, and besides, Claude had the kind of coordination that made tying a shoe difficult. So Slaven beat him about the ears and unshorn beard without mercy, all of it ending as suddenly as it had begun, with the ice cream cone a squashed mess on the sidewalk and Slaven walking away with a certain kind of arrogance and swagger and Claude wiping the blood off his mouth and shaking his fists in the air and shouting, "You sombitch! You sombitch worse than the Japanzees!"

Nobody ever tried to figure out where Claude had found out about the Japanese. But by God, Slaven Budd was responsible for the Rape of Nanking as far as Claude was concerned. Of course, Claude likely thought Nanking was in Benton County.

And then, the year before the war broke out in earnest, with me long gone to the county seat, the ladies of the Methodist Church tried to really dig in and save Slaven Budd's soul. I heard all about it from my Aunt Winifred, who was one of the ladies involved in the saving.

They got him to Sunday school just once because I think Slaven thought there might be something to eat after the lessons. Anyway, he came, bad smell and all, barefooted because this was the dead of summer, and wearing a pair of overalls that had been handed down from Harmon after Harmon figured it was beneath his dignity to clothe himself in such a tattered garment. The dogs came, too. Of course, they didn't get into the Sunday school rooms behind the church, but they found the window where Slaven was sitting just inside and sat down and waited, their tongues hanging out. Now and then one would rise and go wet one of the little church oaks and then come back and take his place with the others.

Unfortunately for Slaven's salvation, a bitch in heat wandered into the group about midway through the discussion of John the Baptist that the parson himself, the Reverend Leviticus Hammel, was conducting for the benefit of about a half dozen well-scrubbed Weedy Rough teenagers. There were those who later said that Leviticus was claiming, like any good Methodist, that a little water sprinkled on the head was just as effective as anything that holy John had done, and that dunking reformed sinners in some local creek until they were half-drowned and wholly waterlogged was not in the spirit of modern times. Maybe it was the wrath of God that came down at that moment in the form of a female dog with biological urgings, right smack in the middle of Slaven's pack of willing he-dogs.

Anyway, the reproductive process began just under the window where Slaven was sitting and watching, and he gave voice to his delight by leaping up and knocking over his chair and hooting, "Gawddamn, look at them dawgs!"

Of course, all the well-scrubbed Weedy Rough youngsters looked, as did Leviticus Hammel, and that was the end of any chance Slaven Budd had for becoming a permanent member of the Methodist Church Sunday school or anything else with which Leviticus Hammel was connected.

But the great moment came the following year for Slaven Budd. He was classified 1-A and ordered to report to Camp Robinson for induction into the army so he could help whip the krauts and the Japs.

It was a little sad for Weedy Roughers, because now they would lose their Budd at the Frisco depot each night when the train came through. Old Harmon had fallen on evil times, what with all his years of drinking and other sins, and so he was pretty well confined to his shack behind the blacksmith shop, where Big Sue took care of him, bringing him mason fruit jars of elderberry wine and cooking up an occasional bait of pinto beans and salt pork.

So after his daddy ceased being a fixture against the trunk of the maple tree at the north end of the depot, Slaven, recognizing his duty to the town, took up the position, although everybody agreed that he wasn't as colorful as his daddy had always been because he had two good legs and he was never drunk and when he decided to cuss, nobody could understand what he was saying.

A lot of people wondered how come Slaven Budd was ever drafted. He wasn't much at reading or writing, but maybe the draft board figured they should at least give him a chance. After all, he'd never had one before.

It was late June and I'd boarded this special coach hooked on to the regular early-morning passenger train at the county seat for about seventy guys, all of us headed for the War. When the train stopped in Weedy Rough, there was Slaven, getting on the train with about three other eighteen-year-olds. The others all carried little suitcases with some personal effects, but Slaven didn't have anything. At least Little Sue had washed his old overalls and starched his denim shirt and he had on shoes. No socks, of course.

There was already a nice little crap game going on in the aisle when Slaven got aboard. And I was there on my knees trying for a nine and a dollar on the line. I gave Slaven a big hello while I rattled the dice in my fist and he nodded and then looked away and didn't even issue a grunt. But he knew me, even though it had been a long time since we'd seen one another. Now and then while the game progressed, all the way to Fort Smith and beyond, Slaven kept cutting these little glances in my direction. Oh, hell yes, he knew me, all right. But he just stood off in one corner of the coach, mostly looking out the window, and I kept wondering what was going through his mind. Here he was riding all the way to Little

Rock, when he'd never in his whole life been farther from Weedy Rough than he could walk in a single day. As far as I knew, he'd never been in an automobile and I knew damned well he'd never ridden a railroad train.

So he just stood there in his corner, cutting those green-eyed glances in my direction now and again.

At Camp Robinson we went through the usual first-day business. Assembly-line induction. They had us strip buck naked, and I could tell it embarrassed Slaven a little. The first thing they did was check us for social diseases—"short-arm inspection," this doctor called it—and when they took a look at Slaven they made him go outside to this big shower and scrub himself off with GI soap. Then they tapped us and probed us and gouged us and finally we formed this long line and started walking past guys standing on either side who popped needles into our arms. I recall there were about six of those pops. Some of the guys passed out cold and had to be dragged out of the way. Slaven didn't pass out. He just blinked a little each time one of those needles went in and he had to have a smallpox vaccination as well, and that didn't bother him either.

I didn't see much of Slaven in the few days I was at Robinson. We were on different routines. I shipped out to Utah for basic training, and all the things that happened to him I heard about after the War.

The army soon found out that Slaven Budd wasn't much for reading or writing or figuring or anything else. He was anxious to do his share, but he just didn't know how. Even the toughest sergeant around had to admit that he wasn't goofing off. So they started to feel sorry for him, all the permanent-party noncommissioned officers who were permanent party because each one of them had some kind of little defect that kept him out of active combat. So they had some sympathy for a guy like Slaven, who had more defects than all of them put together.

His detachment first sergeant used Slaven as a gofer. All

first sergeants have a gofer or two around to run little er-
rands that need running. Go for this, go for that, go here and
there. Hell, Slaven was made for the job!

But eventually the officers discovered Slaven Budd and decided there was no place for him in the army. So they sent him
home with one of those discharges they had then for misfits and queers. Don't blame me for the term *queer*; that's the
word they used then. Of course, it didn't apply to Slaven Budd.
What applied to Slaven Budd was an inability of the army
to understand what a helluva man he would have been with
the K-9 Corps, those guys who handled dogs. But the army
shipped him home because he wasn't much for reading and
writing and figuring and didn't know what toilet paper was for.

It was a big deal when Slaven got off the train in Weedy
Rough, shipped home and out of the War. It was summer, so
his discharge uniform was suntans—spit-shined army shoes
and suntan pants with cutting-edge creases and a suntan shirt.
And somehow he'd gotten away from Camp Robinson with
the true mark of a permanent-party man: a pith helmet! With
a bright brass U.S. Army insignia on the front. He came off
that train, the pith helmet adjusted at a jaunty angle over the
green eyes, and every dog in the county made a beeline for
the Frisco depot.

Those first few days back home must have been intoxicating for Slaven. Joe Sanford gave him all the ice cream cones
he could eat and Dick Page at the drugstore supplied him with
cherry Cokes whenever he wanted one and Esta Stayborn at
his general mercantile sliced off baloney anytime Slaven came
in hungry, all at no cost to the returning hero. You'd have
thought Slaven Budd was Sergeant York. Maybe the town
was trying to make up for all the stuff they'd never done for
him before.

Within a week of his return, Slaven Budd got Weedy Rough
organized for defense. Every kid in town and all the dogs
within sound of his voice he formed into a drill platoon. People stood amazed behind the windows of Olie Merton's bar-

bershop and Bee Shervy's hardware and watched as Slaven ran his organization through their paces. He gave some of the damnedest commands anybody had ever heard. He marched them and counter-marched them up and down the depot platform and out into the street and up onto the new cement sidewalk in front of the post office and in all the places where old Harmon had crawled around screaming and slobbering when somebody hid his peg leg.

It was no longer safe to walk the street in Weedy Rough because you might get entangled in one of Slaven's marching formations. Slaven went about it all with a hardheaded purposefulness that the Reverend Leviticus Hammel would have envied in the saving of souls. He was straight as a ramrod, the pith helmet always slanted down over his eyes, his face cold and calculating, a militant authority it takes a good sergeant half a dozen years to perfect. He never put his hands in his pockets and he never picked his nose when he was giving commands. He was one helluva soldier!

But it started wearing out. As summer left and fall set in, and then winter, and the brown oak leaves were blowing across the Frisco depot platform and the persimmons were turning rust-brown after the first frost and the fox dogs were lifting their voices to the sharp air in all the hills and valleys around the Rough, it started wearing out. The Camp Robinson suntans had accumulated a lot of filth and the crease in the trousers was long since departed and the pith helmet had begun to look a little tattered and the brass insignia had been lost somewhere among the dogs. Slaven's unit fell apart as more and more of the kids deserted because school had started, and then they had to stay home for evening chores. Maybe seeing that their idol had feet of clay and had begun to smell the way he had before he went to the army, even some of the dogs left him.

The first rip in the uniform of the United States Army appeared, naturally, right across his butt and somehow that seemed to take all the dignity out of it.

It went fast after that. By Christmas, Slaven wasn't a soldier anymore. He was just Slaven. By then, he'd even lost the pith helmet somewhere.

When Victory in Europe Day came, Weedy Rough had to celebrate without its most colorful warrior. Before that day, Slaven Budd had gone off, nobody cared to guess where. And I wish I could tell you that he went on to become a man that amounted to something in a far, exotic place where they appreciate a man who talks dog, but I can't. He was boy and man, and then suddenly he wasn't. He was just gone.

And sometimes, even all these years later, when I'm finding it hard to sleep, I wonder about Slaven Budd and all the red and blue and yellow images that must have traveled through his mind. And I wonder what he thought of us while we were thinking so little of him.

And then, without fail, as I lie there in the dark, it happens. From some far place across the next ridge or through a stand of hickory, faint and haunting but as distinct as the etching on a steel plate, a dog barks in the night. And I wonder if Slaven Budd has just passed by.

PART TWO
The County Seat

5

The Last Fastball

Some memories are more painful than others. But like all true raconteurs, Shanks Caulder does not avoid a story just because it has a few thorny patches. In fact, he seems to relish those narratives that illustrate how fragile aspirations and expectations can be, perhaps just to prove that hope can indeed surmount all catastrophes. And then again maybe to prove that hope after some catastrophes really is hopeless.

It was definitely catastrophic when Shanks discovered the fickle nature of love. And just as bad, perhaps even worse, when he realized that he would never become the next Dizzy Dean.

Some guy who has gone to Columbia University or Harvard or some such place and spent his life digging into the human mind, sometimes by watching a lot of rats, is always writing in a book that as we grow older we only recall the good things. They write this particularly about soldiers who have been in various fights around the world, and they claim that after a few years the terrible stuff that happens in a war is forgotten and only the laughing and comradeship is remembered.

This is hogwash. I was a soldier for a long time and I state without reservation that this is hogwash.

It's not true about war, and it's not any truer about what people remember about the rest of their lives.

Take baseball. When we moved from Weedy Rough to the county seat, baseball was the Most Important Thing in Life. To me, that is. What was important to anybody else didn't much concern me.

Even now, after so many seasons without playing a single inning, when summer comes, I can smell neat's-foot oil, which, for the benefit of those who are only basketball followers, is a substance that comes from a cow's foot and is applied to a baseball glove. This is a very, very good memory—just like those guys from Columbia University and Harvard and other such places say we're supposed to have.

But along with that thought comes the vision of Jo Beth York, and for me that's as bad as memory can get.

Jo Beth York came with her family to the county seat about the same time I did, maybe a few weeks later. School had already started, and one day before we'd even learned that some living things reproduced their own kind by doing simple division, Mr. Sylvester Longburn, the school principal, marched her into my home room and stood her at the front of the class and introduced her and said we should all welcome her to the county seat high.

Kirk Elander, one of my close friends and maybe the craziest guy in Washington County, sat right across the aisle from me at the back of the room. When Jo Beth York walked into that room, he fell right out of his seat and lay on the floor making little animal sounds. Because Jo Beth York was the most richly endowed girl he had ever seen. And I had to agree with him.

She was wearing this tight cotton summer dress with little straps over her glorious shoulders where there were a few freckles, and she had bobbed hair that danced when she turned her head, brown and bright as old burnished brass, and her big blue eyes were smiling, along with her beautiful mouth with its little white sweet-corn teeth. This cotton dress was stretched to the point of eruption over a body dominated by what Kirk Elander called "fantastic terrain features," like the Grand Tetons in Wyoming. As a matter of fact, Emmy Joe Gorman, whose real name was Emerick Joseph and whose daddy was city attorney, told me later that the French name for those Wyoming mountains meant precisely what Kirk Elander said it did.

Well, it started something, me seeing Jo Beth York standing in front of the class smiling as confident and brave as Franklin D. Roosevelt the first time he addressed the United Mine Workers of America. What it started was love.

Sometimes you can look back and see the exact moment for something beginning to happen, even though at the time you're just sitting there looking at Jo Beth York with your mouth open and strange things stirring in your chest. Now, all these eons later, I realize that when Mr. Sylvester Longburn walked into that classroom with Jo Beth York, I began to sink into a dismally sticky business.

I guess you'd think as soon as school was out that day, I'd have rushed up to Jo Beth York and tried to persuade her to accompany me on the hayride to the lake the coming Friday night. As a matter of fact, I was afraid to get close to Jo Beth York for almost a year.

After all, here was a girl propelled by rich physical bounty and a lively personality into the center of the most popular groups in high school, among the kids whose parents were members of the country club, and here I was, fresh from the wilderness hills of Weedy Rough and embarrassed by the fact that I had only one pair of decent shoes, and even those had been half-soled three times already.

It's too bad there were none of those old Greek oracles around northwest Arkansas at the time. If there had been, maybe I could have stolen a goat to sacrifice and had a prophecy that would have saved me a lot of trouble. I would have found out this whole thing was going to get very complicated and that baseball would get involved, and a kid named Gret Hogan who lived on the south side of town, and roller skates.

I never owned a pair of roller skates because we couldn't afford them. Jo Beth York had a pair. If I'd known what those roller skates would bring, I could have avoided two years of misery, loving Jo Beth York from afar. So far, in fact, that I wasn't even sure she knew my name.

There were only two things to sop up the goo of my torment. First, there was reading at the library, where my mother had insisted I take out a card as soon as we got to the county seat, showing the great wisdom of mothers. In the library I discovered wonderful things. One of the most wonderful was a book called *Northwest Passage* by some New England guy named Kenneth Roberts. I must have checked that book out fifteen times during my freshman year.

Then one day I went to the library to take out *Northwest Passage* once more, and there on the little checkout card you had to sign was her name: Jo Beth York.

Jesus! I couldn't get through the first chapter because each time I tried to read a line I would think, "Her eyes were on these words!"

I found out later she'd checked the thing out for her mother who was in the hospital recovering from an appendectomy. But before that revelation I gave up *Northwest Passage* for life, just to display my vast devotion to Jo Beth York, though how this was supposed to work wasn't too clear in my mind. I suppose it had something to do with the idea that her reading anything made it sacred.

This didn't affect my reading of textbooks in the classes we had together, because it became quickly apparent from her attempts at recitation and answering the teachers' questions that these were all publications Jo Beth York had never opened.

To set the record straight, I eventually went back on my oath. I started reading *Northwest Passage* again after thirty years. It was better than ever.

The second thing that kept me relatively sane was baseball. Back in those days, baseball came naturally to any kid from a small hill town. What the hell else was there to do? It was part of the culture, a thing I'm not sure those guys from Columbia University and Harvard and other such places ever figured out with their rats.

Back in Weedy Rough, the Fourth of July was always a mighty big deal, mainly because of the afternoon ball game. People came in from all the surrounding hills, mostly in wagons drawn by two mules, and while the old folks sat around the depot discussing politics and how hot it was and how the sorghum cane wasn't doing so good this year and how Mr. Roosevelt had sent all those CCC boys out to Devil's Mountain to build a dam on Blackburn Creek and roads to get to it, the kids would go to Esta Stayborn's or Bee Shirvy's and buy firecrackers.

The kids ran around the dusty street and along the cinders of the Frisco right-of-way, the dogs yammering right along with them and firecrackers going off all over the place, and the mules were braying and the screen door of Joe Sanford's ice cream parlor kept up a constant banging as people went in and out.

The Methodist Ladies' Aid Society always had a big feed of fried chicken and potato salad, which they dished out in the shade of the loading-platform roof at the south end of the depot. They usually had a big pot of Great Northern beans and plenty of lemon pie, too. By a little past noon all the grub was gone and the ladies were cleaning up as the rest of the people started drifting down the road to the ball diamond that lay in a small triangle of flat surface at the base of East Mountain.

About that time a northbound freight always came through, and the ladies cleaning up the mess at the depot loading plat-

form covered their ears as the locomotive roared past within
a few feet of them, and a few of the kids with firecrackers left
threw them at the passing boxcars, and then the train would
be gone and about the only sounds were the jingle of trace
chains on the wagons heading for the ball diamond and a few
blue jays fussing in the pecan tree at Violet Sims's house and
the bleat of Parkins Muller's goats in the hill pasture behind
the telephone central office.

At the ballfield, everything was ready for Esta Stayborn,
the umpire, to yell "Play ball!" Somebody always had a couple of tubs of iced beer hidden in the woods just up the slope
of East Mountain, and there were a few mason jars of white
whiskey in the bib overalls of various citizens.

The women all sat apart from the men, well back in the
trees behind the chickenwire backstop. Grandfather always
took his place on a little knob of ground just behind third
base. As soon as he was seated, the other respectable business men would come sit in a group around him so they could
talk fox racing between innings. I don't know what the women
talked about because I never got back there to that part of the
hillside.

It was usually a pretty good game, with a minimum of fistfights. Me and all the other kids would get impatient as hell
about the sixth inning, wanting the grown-up game to be finished because right afterward we took over the diamond.

We didn't have spectators for our game. All the grownups
went back into town to see Number Six come through, and
then the people from the sticks headed their mules back out
the various roads toward their hill farms and some of the town
men got ready for a fox race and some of the women hurried
home to powder their noses and put on their best Sunday
dresses in preparation for the Eastern Star meeting that night.

It would be approaching full dark by the time we headed
home, dusty and tired and sweat-soaked. It was really wonderful, walking along in little groups, talking about good plays

that had been made and teasing guys about their errors. Maybe the smells were best of all—the dust and the cinders from Number Six, the smoke lying on the still air in the valley, the neat's-foot oil, the sweat, and the lingering odor of burnt powder from firecrackers. It smelled like the Fourth of July. It smelled like baseball.

Well, that's the way it smelled in Weedy Rough, anyway. It wasn't quite the same in the county seat, but at least there was plenty of it.

What amazed me most was that almost every house had a radio, a Philco or a Brunswick or one of those others, so they could pick up the broadcasts of the St. Louis Cardinals. Everybody rooted for the Cardinals. Especially after the '34 season, when Dizzy Dean and his brother Paul won fifty games between them, and then the Red Birds beat Detroit in a seven-game World Series.

Olie Merton almost got himself arrested right after that Series. Some traveling soda-cracker salesman made the claim one day that the Dean boys were actually from Oklahoma instead of Arkansas, and Olie beat hell out of him with a razor strop before the guy could escape from Olie's shop. Olie was a town hero.

Baseball was a serious thing before the War, like football got to be later. But it was better than football because you didn't have to have all that leather upholstery on your head to keep from getting your skull caved in or an ear torn off. All you needed was the old fielder's glove your Uncle Jack or somebody had discarded, a scuffed-up ball, a couple of taped Louisville Slugger bats, and a piece of flat ground big enough to lay out a diamond.

Anyway, just like Weedy Rough, the county seat was nuts over baseball. I was happy to discover this, but it still didn't smell the same.

There were two grade schools in the county seat. The one on the north side was Washington and the one on the south side was Jefferson, obviously named for the first and third presidents of the United States. John Adams didn't figure into it, I guess because the people figured if a guy was leader of his country and still didn't get his picture on the money, he didn't deserve to have a school named after him, either.

Each school had a sandlot baseball team. But that was just the farm system. Those same guys went right on playing after they got into high school, sometimes for four years, and they still called themselves the Washingtons and the Jeffersons. These were tough ball clubs. They had guys sixteen and seventeen years old, and they didn't spend a lot of time booting ground balls around on the infield.

There was an American Legion team in town, too. But most of the boys didn't go out for that because the south-side guys usually started working as soon as they left grade school and didn't have time, and the north-side guys mostly thought they were too damned high-toned to have some old man manager yelling at them all the time. Besides, that Legion team had guys like Sherman Lollar playing for them, and you know how good he was—he ended up as the regular catcher for the Chicago White Sox. He was not only a great ballplayer, but a helluva nice guy.

My first year in the county seat, I started playing for the Washingtons because we lived on the north side. It was an accident of geography. We had this little rented house at the base of Mount Sidney, where the Senator's mother lived. Actually, I really belonged on the south side because we sure as hell were not a part of the country-club set. Unlike most of the kids on the Washingtons, I worked five days a week and during the summer, labeling cans of tomatoes and loading the boxes on cars in a Frisco railroad siding warehouse.

It's really crazy that I still like to eat canned tomatoes. I worked beside this old bastard who had a crusty neck like he'd varnished it years before and the varnish was beginning to peel off. I hated his guts.

The old clout spent most of his time in the warehouse leaning against a stack of tomato cases, picking his teeth with the long blade of a bone-handled pocketknife. While I was working my butt off and sweating a river, this lovely was just leaning and picking and talking to the two old ladies who sat at this long table slapping paste and labels on cans. He always told off-color stories, like maybe he thought these two old ladies were going to start squealing and throw themselves on him. Fat chance.

Anyway, his favorite story, and one I heard about seven million times, was about his little mongrel dog. This dog came into his seed time, see, and started trying to mount everything in sight. Depraved, this old son of a bitch said, trying to hump such things as the neighbor's cat, chunks of firewood, and sofa pillows. The final embarrassment was when this dork's little mutt sexually assaulted a piece of burlap hanging on the chicken coop fence. So right then, he always explained in bloody detail, out came his trusty pocketknife and with a quick slice he reduced the dog's prospects of progeny.

And I figured he went right back to picking his teeth with the same blade.

Jesus, I hated that son of a bitch.

And in all the time I sweated beside him in that Frisco warehouse, I never heard him mention baseball. I don't think he even knew who the St. Louis Cardinals were. What a dyed-in-the-wool ignorant bastard! Not even knowing who the Cardinals were, and cutting off a little dog's nuts just because of nature.

Well, anyway, there I was in my first year in the county seat and playing for the Washingtons. There was good reason they wanted me. Most of the girls in the Weedy Rough school could outrun me. My hitting consisted of punching little Texas League singles over second base. Handling hot ground balls on the infield scared me to death. I was a fair outfielder.

But mostly, I was a chucker.

The Washingtons had this little sprout named Johnny
Salmon who was their regular pitcher. He was a lefty. He had
this slow, lazy curve that drove a batter crazy, taking so long
to get to the plate you could recite half the Lord's Prayer by
the time it squished into the catcher's mitt. Youth being im-
petuous, those Jefferson batters would be swinging from the
heels before the nugget got halfway to the plate.

But the Washingtons had been taking a beating almost
every game, because after about six innings even the most
impatient batter would finally figure out the timing and then
he'd wait for Johnny's curve and plaster it all over the lot, and
so the Jeffersons usually won it in the last three innings.

That is, until I arrived.

Without trying to be too damned modest about it, I threw
nothing but smoke. I had this fastball that came in like a gar-
den-variety black-eyed pea and, about three feet in front of
the plate, took a sudden fade in toward a right-handed hitter.
Or away from a left-handed hitter, you see? So Johnny would
pitch the first six innings and then I'd come in from the outfield and start buzzing them past everybody. Just when they'd
adjusted to Johnny's little fluttery curve, they got to see it
coming at them like an aspirin shot out of a deer rifle.

Hell, if I didn't strike out at least six of the last nine batters, I figured it was a bad day.

The one player the Jeffersons had that I really enjoyed vic-
timizing was Gret Hogan. I guess he was a nice enough kid,
but he was supposed to be their big gun. He played center
field and was as tall as me but a lot heavier. He had straight
black hair and strange eyes and we all figured he was part Indian. Anyway, when Gret Hogan came up, I really bore
down, and through that first summer I played with the Washingtons, I struck him out every time he came near a bat.

It was just a wonderful year, even if it did smell different.
And the greatest thing that had yet happened in my life hit me
that summer like a load of butterscotch ice cream. Only
sweeter.

It was Labor Day weekend and we were going against the Jeffersons for the last time that summer. After I'd come in from the outfield to relieve Johnny in the seventh, and had run through the first three batters like a hungry dog in the packing house, who comes walking up in our half of the eighth but a bunch of high school girls, and right in the middle of them is Jo Beth York!

How can you describe something like that? We played on one of the intramural fields at the local college, and those girls stood in a tight group with Jo Beth York looking like heaven itself with the windows of the Law School building behind her reflecting the late sunlight. She was golden and bright and the Grand Tetons and she was doing more watching than talking, as though she knew a little about this game, and she was looking at me and I was cutting down Jefferson hitters like I had a machine gun.

She was watching my ball game, and everybody in town knew her parents, and she was just back from seeing the New York World's Fair. Jo Beth York had been to the World's Fair, and here I was—I'd never been any farther away from northern Arkansas than Kansas City—and she was watching me pitch. After seeing that big white ball and that big white needle in Flushing Meadow, a thing most of the rest of us had only seen in *Life* magazine and the Pathé newsreel at the Palace Theater.

It was better than anything. It was better than going to the College Theater one night with my mother and seeing a moving-picture show called *Goodbye Mr. Chips* with some guy named Robert Donat, and not really seeing a damned minute of it because I knew Jo Beth was sitting with her mother and daddy just three rows in front of us. She hadn't looked back at me once.

But now, that September afternoon on a Labor Day weekend, there were the Grand Tetons watching me throw a baseball, which I knew I did pretty well.

Well, we beat hell out of the Jeffersons that afternoon, and afterward everybody came up and was slapping me on the back and saying, "Great game. Great game."

Hell, I knew that. I looked and the sun had sunk far enough so the windows in the Law School building were no longer golden, and the girls had gone, and as I walked the seventeen blocks home carrying my glove and my bat, I told myself that most likely Jo Beth York had said something to the effect that with this guy pitching, meaning me, the issue was no longer in doubt. So why hang around?

If she was impressed, she sure didn't act like it a few days later when school started. We only had one class together and she treated me like shit. Worse than that. She acted as though I wasn't even there. I was so low I couldn't even get charged up when she got the right answer to a question the teacher asked. We had this textbook on world history that had been written by somebody from the University of Chicago, and when the teacher asked her where that was, she got it right. Later, Kirk Elander said Jo Beth York was becoming the intellectual giant of the county seat high school. I felt as sorry for her as I did for myself.

That fall and winter went on forever, like Mr. Gibbon's book on the decline and fall of the Roman Empire. I got another edition of half-soles on my good shoes, and the big deal at Christmas was a present of rubber overshoes that were supposed to protect the new half-soles, I suppose. I needed them that winter because it seemed to snow more than usual, but maybe that was just because I was feeling dismal and the whole world around me seemed cold and heartless.

At noon hour when I was despondent, I'd go to Rufus Blair's little store across the street from the high school to eat my baloney sandwich and smoke a cigarette and try to work up some high spirits by laughing with the football players when they told dirty jokes.

Rufus had a large wineglass on his candy counter, and it was filled with Chesterfield cigarettes that cost a penny each.

That was a long time before everybody started telling us that smoking cigarettes would not only stain our fingers yellow but would put us in an early grave.

A lot of my friends were playing basketball and I was in the band at each game, honking the trombone. I don't think Jo Beth York came to a single one of those games, and believe me, I always looked.

That was the winter Kirk Elander introduced me to his own special type of bootleg liquor. He called it Skim-Blim. It was half grain alcohol and half grape juice. He always threw in a few handfuls of sugar or salt or something—I was never sure what—and it would turn your socks purple.

Some Saturday nights I'd make an excuse to get out of the house and hitch a ride to the Lilac Club, north of town on the federal highway. I'd have a dollar in my pocket from sacking groceries at the Kroger on the town square. I liked going to the Lilac Club so I could hear Emmy Joe Gorman's stepdaddy play in the band. Usually, the fights in the parking lot were even more fun than watching girls dance over the light that was set in the middle of the floor and gave all the watching guys a pretty good idea of the kind of legs they had.

Jo Beth York sure as hell never came to the Lilac Club.

In the county seat they had this high school fraternity called the Delta Sigma, and that winter they asked me to join. It was a bright spot in a gloomy season. All my friends were already members, and Emmy Joe Gorman was president. It was nice to know that somebody wanted you in their club. But my mother was working hard to put three kids through school and we didn't have any money for luxuries, which included initiation fees to a high school frat.

These guys had dances and parties and all kinds of good stuff and held meetings each Sunday afternoon at the Washington Hotel, where they wore suits and ties and shook hands with one another and acted like they were members of the state legislature. And they wore expensive little gold pins on their shirts. All the girls thought the Delts were keen, elite, and rich, and it was a major accomplishment for a girl to get "pinned," which meant that some Delt guy asked her to wear his pin.

All through the winter, when I walked into world history class, the first thing I did was look at Jo Beth York's impressive front to see if one of those little gold pins was attached there. It never was, which I guess was a plus on my ledger.

A lot of guys who weren't Delts felt like second-class citizens. I know I did, even though I'd been asked. Down through the years, I've often wondered what kind of agony it must have been for a lot of kids who were never even invited to join. Like you weren't worth anything, like you didn't count.

By the time I was a senior, I'd saved enough money to join, so I did and put on that little gold pin and felt like something special. I was just the same guy, but that little pin made me different, above the common mold.

It took a lot of years, but I finally decided that the whole business was cruel and unusual punishment for about ninety-five percent of the guys in high school. And that the whole idea of high school frats and select clubs and snooty organizations should be counted at least a second-degree misdemeanor.

Thank God for the moving-picture shows that winter. There were some great ones. Emmy Joe Gorman and me went to see *Gone With the Wind* three times. And my taste buds hadn't been affected by Jo Beth York. The chicken salad sandwiches at the smoke shop and the ten-cent bowls of chili at the Castle Lunch were enough to make a guy forget even Bette Davis in *Jezebel* or Ginger Rogers in *Kitty Foyle*.

Finally, it came around again. Baseball season!

And roller skates!

Actually, the county seat wasn't a very good place for roller skates. There weren't many sidewalks and the streets were pretty narrow and most of them sharp up and down, what with the hills the town was built on. But Jo Beth York had a pair, with those little ball bearings as deadly as buckshot, I found out.

It was leaf-out time, when everything was going so green it almost hurt your eyes. I'd just finished doing a little job for a lady on Willow Street, trimming some of her dogwood trees, and was walking along toward home, thinking about neat's-foot oil and getting out a couple of old baseballs I had and restitching the covers on them. I wasn't even thinking about walking right past the York house until I heard somebody calling me.

So I turned around and there she was, standing in a pair of roller skates that looked like they were made out of sterling silver, holding on to the door handle of the garage about twenty feet from the street up a steep concrete driveway.

"Come catch me, Shanks!" she yelled. "I wanta roll down the driveway!"

Jesus!

I dropped the pruning shears on the spot and ran over, and almost before I got positioned, Jo Beth York released her hold on the garage door handle and was coming right at me down that driveway. I grabbed her and my arms were around her and I felt the Grand Tetons against me and her arms were around me and she was laughing. And then she kissed me. Right on the mouth!

It wasn't any big deal. Like no more than a 155 howitzer shell exploding inside my head.

"Pull me back up," Jo Beth York said.

So I pulled her up and she held on to the garage door handle until I got back down at the far end of the driveway and she came again. And this time her mouth was all over me before I even had a good hold on her.

"Let's go in now," she said, panting a little.

We went into her mother's living room and she pushed me

down on this couch and was right beside me and her arms were around me and she started kissing me again.

"Where's your mother?" I asked.

"Shopping," she said, and put her face tight against mine.

My God. Up to that time in my life I'd always liked moving-picture shows because there was sometimes some shooting and other action and when the kissing and squeezing started, I'd eat my popcorn and think maybe it was a good time to go to the john. But now, with Jo Beth York, I'm Clark Gable. With Constance Bennett. Or Irene Dunne. Or Jean Harlow.

I don't know how long it went on, because I was in a trance. Just like Leslie Howard with Vivien Leigh. Then suddenly Jo Beth York said I had to go because her mother was about to get home. I don't know how she timed it so close. But I cut out of there like I'd been caught stealing the family silver. And sure enough, when I'm picking up the pruning shears, there's Mrs. York pulling into that same driveway where the kissing had started and smiling at me and taking out a bag of groceries from the backseat of the car.

I ran all the way home. With a few jumps thrown in between steps. Nothing like that had ever happened to me. And there was some kind of thing running inside me. Like a roaring river, man.

Well, it all became a big secret. I never afterward told Kirk Elander or Emmy Joe Gorman about it because I knew what they'd ask: "Hey, man, where were your hands? All that kissin' and did you explore the Grand Tetons?"

Hell, I couldn't do anything dirty with the body of Jo Beth York. So my hands were always on her shoulders while she was slobbering all over my mouth.

So it was a big secret. And I knew it was, because Jo Beth York acted as though it had never happened. It was a special thing between us. That's how I had it figured. I walked around with a bounce. And right after the kissing, baseball season was there and we had our first game with the Jeffersons not two weeks after Jo Beth York and me did our Scarlet-and-Rhett act on her mother's couch.

A little sour note crept in on the Friday before the game. First, it was raining cats and dogs and I was worried it wouldn't stop, and even if it did, the diamond would be muddy as hell and maybe the game wouldn't be played. I was going into the third-floor study hall, worrying about the rain, when Pepper Winnington came up to me, grinning, and he had this little bit of silk fluff in his hand.

"You know what this is?" he asked, and when I said no, he snickered. "It's a pair of Jo Beth's step-ins."

I knew it was Pepper's idea of a joke and that probably those panties belonged to one of his younger sisters, but it just made me crazy. I beat hell out of him right there at the front of the study hall and books were flying in all directions and Pepper was laughing like a crazy man each time I hit him and there was blood all over his shirt. I might have killed him if Miss Simpson, the school librarian, hadn't pulled me off. My good friend Pepper, and there I'd opened up his face just because of a little fun he was trying to have.

They wanted to kick me out of school even though the semester was almost over, so my mother went down and talked to Mr. Sylvester Longburn, the principal, and tried to explain that I wasn't a bloodthirsty Hun. So he said there was the little matter of some of the words I'd used, to the detriment of freshman morals, in case any freshmen had been listening, and my mother said she couldn't imagine where I'd learned such language.

They let me stay in school to complete my final exams, but I could have told them that when Pepper Winnington pulled that panties routine on me, I *had* been a Hun thirsting for blood.

Pepper giggled about it for two or three months, but during that time he looked like he had a harelip from where my fists had sliced him. Damn! My good friend and I'd done that to him. I felt pretty bad about the whole thing. But I never apologized to the son of a bitch.

Anyway, the rain stopped, so on Saturday we all gathered at the college intramural field. The pitcher's mound was a little gummy, but other than that, it was okay. The sun was out in a clear blue sky and there were some college students hurrying past with books in their hands, it being final exam time.

Some honeysuckle was growing up one side of the home-plate backstop and it was in bloom and smelled great, and Kirk Elander had a big brown grocery bag full of roasted peanuts that he'd swiped from some vendor at the county fair a couple of weeks before, and everybody was tossing goobers into their mouths while we did our warmup.

Johnny Salmon started the game and he was going good, that southpaw curve of his looping in there and making the Jefferson batters look like fools. I was in right field enjoying the view and not getting any action, and about the fifth inning the girls arrived.

There must have been fifteen or twenty of them and Jo Beth York right in amongst them, wearing a little bare-shouldered sun dress, flame red. I beat my fist into my glove and started my loud chatter as the girls moved up behind the backstop, where they could cheer for both sides without prejudice.

In the seventh, Johnny got two Jeffersons out, but then a couple of them got singles so they had a runner on first and third. Johnny gave me the sign and I went in to the mound and he handed me the ball.

"Watch out for Gret Hogan," Johnny said. "I hear he's told it around he's gonna blast you out of here if you keep throwing those fastballs."

"Yeah? Well, we'll see about Gret Hogan," I said.

I struck out the next Jefferson batter and that ended the threat. So we were at six to five, a one-run lead for the Washingtons, and nothing to worry about.

We went into the bottom of the ninth with the score unchanged. I got the first guy on a little pop to third. The next guy I struck out. And then there was Gret Hogan, waving a big black bat and coming up to the left side of the plate. I grinned at him and he grinned at me. We didn't need the girls yelling from behind the backstop to know it was on the line, right here and now.

Gret hogged the plate a little, so I figured I'd brush him back. And with that tailing fastball of mine that faded off to the right, it might make him jump back and then cut a corner of the plate for a called strike.

I gave it that old-time windmill windup and kicked my left foot up and blazed it. But even when that ball left my fingers, I knew something was wrong. My left foot had skidded a little in the mud around the rubber. The ball went like a shot, higher than I wanted, and it didn't tail away. It kept right on going for Gret Hogan's head, and I knew he wasn't fast enough to get out of the way.

It caught him just above the right ear, and his ball cap went sailing and the ball arced up in the air like it was a pop foul and Gret went down like a limp potato sack. There are few sounds more sickening than a baseball hitting a guy in the head.

All hell broke loose. The Jeffersons ran over to Gret, who was flopping around on the ground like a neck-wrung chicken, and the girls were right behind them, screaming, waving their hands. Everybody but my own guys were yelling about what a dyed-in-the-wool butcher I was, and there were threats of bodily harm to me and all my family. I just stood there on the mound, wondering what the hell had happened to that pitch.

They got Gret back to their bench, the girls helping and Jo Beth York helping most of all with her hands on him, and shooting glares out toward me that would have withered a grape. But good little Johnny Salmon had run all the way in from right field to stand there beside me.

"Jesus Christ, Shanks, I didn't think you'd bean the son of a bitch just because of what he said."

"What's the matter with you?" I said. "I didn't hit him on purpose."

I hate to talk about the rest of it. Things finally got settled down, only now the girls were all behind the Jeffersons' bench and the time for unprejudiced yelling was over and it sounded like everybody wanted my scalp. Most of all Jo Beth York, who was right behind Gret, her hands on his shoulders, and Gret slumped on the bench with his eyes glassy and a big knot coming up purple and black above his right ear.

They put a pinch-runner on first and sent this scrawny little hitter out to the plate whose name I didn't even know and I was thinking about the sound of the ball against Gret's skull and this little guy hit my first pitch.

I didn't have to look. I knew from the sound and the way that ball came off the stick. I just walked off the field to pick up my bat and get the hell home. The girls were screaming and the Jeffersons were screaming and I knew Johnny Salmon out in right field was still chasing the ball after both runs crossed the plate and we'd lost seven to six.

Nobody said a word to me. My own guys were stunned, just standing out there on the diamond, stunned. The Jeffersons and the girls were going crazy. I didn't look back. And my arm had begun to hurt like hell.

It was seventeen long blocks home, and every step of the way I thought about Jo Beth York with her hands on Gret Hogan. And I thought about that skinny little bastard who'd blasted my pitch so far into right field it was more like artillery practice than baseball.

That night I lay in my bed trying to put the image out of my mind: Jo Beth York showing off her roller skates to Gret Hogan and inviting him in to inspect her mother's living room couch when her mother was grocery shopping.

Lucky for me, it was a busy summer. Emmy Joe Gorman

had a lot of things going on, like teaching me to fence with a set of foils his stepdaddy had bought him. And I went to a band seminar in Little Rock, sponsored by the Boys' Club. And Kirk Elander and me brewed a little Skim-Blim, and a couple of times we slipped into the city park swimming pool after it had closed and took a buck-naked dip. And I went down to Weedy Rough a few times to visit Grandfather and watch their team play West Fork.

I didn't go out anymore with the Washingtons. It wasn't their fault. It was me. I just didn't feel like it. I kept saying my arm hurt. And I could still hear the sound of that ball hitting Gret Hogan's head. I can still hear it.

And Jo Beth York?

Well, it didn't take me long to get over her. About ten years is all. But the hard sting went away by October when the trees started turning red and gold and the town started smelling like burning elm leaves and the football guys at Rufus Blair's store had a bunch of new jokes and cigarettes were still a penny each.

My good friends like Pepper and Kirk and Emmy Joe razzed me a little. But I'd just shake my head and laugh with them. It wasn't a brutal razzing. It was no big deal. Now and then they'd look at me out of the corners of their eyes and say, "Grand Tetons." That's when I'd just shake my head and laugh with them.

I never have cared a helluva lot for Wyoming since that summer of 1940. And things were happening then that would make baseball and Jo Beth York and almost everything else of no account. Things were happening then that would sweep us all up and into things where nobody cared whether you could control your fastball or not.

6

Raised in
the Wilderness

Afterward, only a few of the older ones remembered Audie Renkin and the violence in the snow.

It all happened just before the young men, including Shanks, went off to Kasserine Pass and Guadalcanal and Anzio and Peleliu.

Though there aren't many around who remember, Shanks does. Remembering is his profession now. It may not be much of a profession, but it's all Shanks Caulder's got, and he's happy with it.

Shanks admits that he can turn memory on and off like a faucet. He's what might be called a selective historian, which means he's not really a historian at all. That suits him just fine.

Everybody who knows Shanks has come to realize there are some faucets he can't turn off. It's just a matter of how long he can stand their dripping before he lets go and just starts talking about it.

Take that Renkin case. Every November, after the green has gone, after the hardwoods have lost all but the most stubborn leaves, after the fields are lying dormant and the

115

cardinals have stopped singing, after a week or so of silver frost on the rails of the Frisco line each morning, Shanks remembers the Renkins. Without willing it, perhaps. Maybe even fighting it, but knowing he'll be defeated in the end and have to tell the story once more as a sort of confessional that will give him absolution over the cold months ahead, not that he has ever consciously felt that he needed absolution for anything.

Often, it's been noted, Shanks drives to the city of Tadmor just to pass by the old Blue Moon Café. It's not called that anymore. It's an abstract office now. But it's the same building, and as Shanks drives by in his old Plymouth he can still see in his mind the black bloodstains in the cracks of the mosaic floor.

Then he heads back to his general mercantile store in the hills, takes his place among the rat traps and whiskbrooms, and thinks about it a while before he begins to tell it once more.

It always starts the same way.

"You know," Shanks says, "the Renkin boys were both born in November. The same month as the trouble."

"Yeah," somebody says. "My wife tells me it's all in the stars. Them Scorpio people. Give you their last dime if you're for 'em. Sting your ass if you ain't."

"Well," says Shanks, "I don't know about that. I was born in November, you know."

"You'd give me your last dime, wouldn't you, Shanks?"

"Depending on your collateral."

"Well, my wife admits it don't work on everybody."

The exact year don't matter. What matters is it was before the War and I was a sophomore in high school at the county seat and I'd never seen a murder trial before. In fact, I'd never seen any kind of trial before.

One day in the spring, when the whole town smelled of cut grass and the mockingbirds were going crazy and the wild plum trees were like pink powder puffs and the idea of cutting classes was pretty strong anyway, Emmy Joe Gorman came up to me during second-period study hall and said there was a helluva trial going on downtown and why didn't we just skip school for the rest of the day and go down there and listen to Winthrop Scadins try to keep this guy out of the electric chair.

I might point out that in those times guys were sent to the electric chair on a frequent basis. Not as frequent as old Judge Parker once sent them to the rope from that federal court in Fort Smith, but often enough for it not to be a big deal in the newspapers and on the television. Of course, there wasn't any television then. But whatever.

Winthrop Scadins was the most famous criminal lawyer in this part of the country then. He was a little guy who looked like he'd just finished teaching a class in freshman algebra and still had the chalk dust on his clothes. Nobody called him Winthrop, of course. They called him Rex. Beats hell out of me why.

Anyway, Rex Scadins was a good friend of Emmy Joe's stepdaddy, who was city attorney then. Rex played a very mean jazz fiddle. He played it every Saturday night at a place called the Lilac Club, which looked like a one-story tarpaper barracks and was out on the highway north of the county seat. You had to pay a quarter to get in, and nobody checked your age, and then another fifteen cents for a bottle of Falstaff, and then you had to stand in line at the one-position john. The Lilac Club was something. But that's another story. In fact, that's a lot of other stories.

So Rex Scadins was defending this guy for killing a few people, and me and Emmy Joe cut school and went to the courthouse and saw the final part and the closing arguments. Ever since that day I have figured that our court system is pretty good, even though it's more a stage play than anything else, and more fun than the annual high school operetta ever was, but without the singing.

The thing that took some of the fun out of it for me was it started me thinking about justice. I've thought about it ever since. What I finally decided is that I don't know much about

it, and I doubt anybody else does. I guess justice is whatever
twelve folks on a jury say it is, although sometimes there is
a judge here and there who thinks he needs to instruct them.
Not about the details of the law, you understand, but about
justice. But it seems to me those twelve people on a jury
know as much about justice as anybody, so long as none of
them are drunk or crazy, because they've had plenty of experience in everyday life at seeing how it don't work.

Anyway, the guy getting tried for all this homicide was
named Audie Renkin. He was one of those yellow-eyed hill
boys you used to see a lot of around here before the Yankees
and lowlanders started coming into the hills to build retire-
ment homes with Jacuzzis, encroaching on the native population. He had straw-colored hair always cut short, and a long
face with flat features that looked like they had been planed
out of a slab of Ozark limestone, and were pretty much the
same color except for the pink across his cheeks. He was tall
and hard-boned and tough. But they tell me he always said
"ma'am" and "sir" to his elders, which you don't find much
of anymore.

Audie came from a family of hill farmers near Weedy
Rough. Audie's pap died a little while after Audie's oldest
brother, Hoadie, had been killed trying to rob a bank. That
was Depression times, see, and in this part of the country
there were a lot of guys going around robbing a bank here and
there. So you can see this family was not one of the country-
club set.

When Old Man Renkin died, Audie and his brother Cecil
stayed on the farm long enough to bury him and then waited
two days for an uncle to come pick up their mama and the
other kids. There were nine other kids, ranging in age from
twelve to six months. This guy wasn't really an uncle but they
called him that because he was always there when the old
man was out someplace on a fox hunt or dead drunk or both.
This uncle arrived almost before the old man was cold in his

grave, as though he might have been hiding in the woods behind the house, biding his time, and he made his proposition.

Old Lady Renkin accepted the uncle's plan to move off
with him to some rock farm in Crawford County because I
guess she figured anything would be better than the way she'd
been living for twenty-five years, trying to grub a few tomatoes and corn from a hillside field.

It was likely that Audie and Cecil were never able to figure
out why any sane man would be so hot to bed their mother
on a continuing basis that he'd be willing to take on those nine
kids into the bargain. But they were too young to understand
true love coupled with a dash of pure animal lust. Audie was
only twenty-one then, and barely able to read and write his
own name.

So after they'd laid their pap down and seen their mama off
in a wagon drawn by two brindle mules, Audie took Cecil and
the only livestock that was left, two bitch foxhounds, and a
double-barrel Ithaca shotgun and started north. He sold the
dogs and the shotgun in Weedy Rough for seventeen dollars,
all told, and him and Cecil rode the rods on a Frisco freight
train as long as they could stand it and got off—in Tadmor,
all of forty miles from where they'd started.

For a while they lived on handouts from houses along the
railroad at Tadmor. There were a lot of men on the move
then, and they kept from starving by knocking on back doors
and saying they'd do some work for a meal—stack the firewood, cut the weeds, clean out the cow stall. The lady of the
house would give them a couple of cold biscuits with a slather
of French's mustard and a chunk of fried salt pork left over
from breakfast.

That's a good sandwich, baking-soda biscuits and mustard
and crisp fried salt pork. But don't look for it on any menus
in New York or San Francisco.

However they did it, the boys sort of grew up with the town
of Tadmor. This was the early thirties, and fruit growing and
canning and trucking were holding their own and getting bet-

ter, even with the Depression, and I guess those two boys worked at all sorts of things and finally ended up driving little bob trucks, hauling produce to Muskogee and Tulsa and Joplin and Monet and places like that.

Tadmor was some town! Most of the people there thought the name came from the eighth chapter of Second Chronicles where it tells about old King Solomon building cities. One was Tadmor, raised in the wilderness.

I always knew better because I had a great-great-granddaddy on my mother's side who helped found the place. You might have to throw in a couple more greats, because this was back in 1840. His name was Quinton, and him and Ulysses X. Tadmor came into this country from Kentucky and started a Primitive Baptist church, and the town just naturally grew up around it. And was named after Ulysses X. History doesn't record what the X stood for, but it must have been some Greek word meaning "fruitful," because Ulysses X. planted the first orchards and vineyards there, and they gave forth their bounty. And besides that, he sired twenty-seven children by various wives who weren't as tough as he was and kept dying off after the sixth or seventh baby was born.

My ancestor Quinton and Ulysses would never have recognized the place at the time Audie Renkin came. There was a federal highway, and roads going out in all directions to the fields and orchards and vineyards, and a railroad. Before the War, I can remember those little roadside stands where they sold Concord grapes, big and purple and sweet. Little roadside stands that looked like discarded penny matchboxes. It wasn't much for pretty, but those grapes and peaches and apples and green beans and tomatoes and watermelons! God! What ever happened to things that taste like that?

So the time came. That November was a cold one, like we get around here now and again. There'd been a week or more of low clouds, gray as coaldust and threatening snow, when the poker game began. They played where they always did, this bunch of big spenders, in a back room on the second floor of the Tadmor Hotel, where Main Street crossed the Frisco tracks.

It wasn't much of a hotel. Each room had the same stuff. A double bed with those old-fashioned cast-iron bedsteads where you could stick your chewing gum before you went to sleep at night. There must have been a quarter-ton of old chewing gum in the Tadmor Hotel. Remember that old tune called "Does the Spearmint Lose Its Flavor on the Bedpost Overnight?" Whoever wrote that epic must have been thinking about the Tadmor Hotel.

Besides the bed, there was a bureau with most of the drawer handles broken off, a frayed easy chair upholstered in puke green, and a bare forty-watt light bulb hanging from the ceiling on a yellow electric cord. A real class place.

In the room they used for poker playing, there was a round table and enough straight-back chairs to accommodate seven hopefuls. Clarence Stoddard, who ran the place, never rented the poker room to overnight truckers or railroaders, keeping it vacant in case the town sharks found an unexpected visitor from Missouri or Illinois who had a wallet full of money and nothing to do with his time until the next passenger train came through.

But the time Audie Renkin played, there were no Missouri or Illinois guys. It was just the local bunch that always came together on the first and fifteenth of each month, when the canning factories and trucking outfits made their payrolls.

The game started on Thursday, about noon, and lasted until Saturday night. Clarence Stoddard brought up potato salad and barbecued ribs now and then. Or a jug of black homemade wine or a fifth or two of Old Crow and some bottles of soda for chasers. And just about anything the players wanted except women, because this was a serious game and besides that, Clarence Stoddard had some ideas of his own about morals.

Sometimes it got pretty smoky, what with cigars and cigarettes going all the time, and noisy as well with freight trains passing just below the windows and the trucks coming in from farms with crates of turkeys for the grocery-store meat markets for Thanksgiving. Fresh birds for Turkey Day then, not this frozen crap you get now.

The guys would take catnaps on the double bed, snoozing among the wads of dried and hardened chewing gum, then come back into the game bleary-eyed and wanting a drink and a good fistful of cards.

A lot of money changed hands, according to testimony later. Then, about three A.M. on Saturday, it stopped changing hands and started piling up on the table in front of Audie Renkin.

There were a lot of rumors about Audie cheating in that game. But Emmy Joe Gorman said whoever heard of some hill-farmer hick who knew how to palm aces? Besides, Emmy Joe said, they were playing mostly five-card stud, a game anybody with a little luck and a lot of card sense could reckon his chances pretty close. Especially in a game that ran for over fifty hours, where a man had plenty of time to see how other guys played their cards. And where, toward the end, the other guys were exhausted or drunk or both. And in everything we ever heard about Audie Renkin, he never got exhausted or drunk either.

From my own penny-ante experience, I've found that the closest to a sure-thing poker game you can get is one where you stay sober while all the other guys are sucking a bottle between each deal.

Anyway.

Audie Renkin won about twenty thousand dollars. Maybe more. Probably less. The exact amount was never established at the trial, but it was damned sure a hunk of real money at that time, the tag end of the Great Depression.

So, late on Saturday afternoon, Audie said he'd had enough and was pulling out of the game. Clarence Stoddard was in the room at the time, having just brought up a brown poke of hamburgers, the grease turning the bottom of the sack wet and smelling like only real hamburgers can smell. He said at the trial that when Audie told them he was out, they made some very rude and abrupt remarks and said that Audie Renkin wasn't leaving no game until he'd given them a chance to win back their money—the usual wail made by losers.

But Audie Renkin pulled on his overcoat and walked out, every pocket stuffed with currency.

It had been snowing most of the afternoon, and when Audie left the hotel there was a soft cover of white on everything and all the sounds were muted in the flakes that were still coming down like fat confetti. Even that tawdry old Main Street in Tadmor must have looked like a three-dollar Christmas card and lifted Audie's spirits.

Audie had a little trouble starting his 1931 LaSalle sedan. He'd bought it just the month before from a guy who claimed it had belonged to a Chicago gangster, and there was a bullet hole in the right rear fender to prove it. A .38-caliber hole. Everybody said a 1931 LaSalle with a Chicago bullet hole was just what a guy like Audie Renkin needed to make him feel like he was finally out of the backwoods timber and making his way in civilization.

He drove to the little three-room house he'd rented about six months earlier, and picked up the lady who'd been living with him there from the day he moved in. Before the War, unmarried couples didn't do a lot of living together right out in the open, like they later got into the habit of doing. They transacted their writhing and wiggling and sweating in the backseat of a car or else in some remote tourist court, which is what they called motels then, and there were a lot of citizens who said that Audie Renkin had brought his hound-dog morals with him from Weedy Rough, being so obvious about what most folks had the decency to keep secret.

Audie Renkin and his lady, whose name was Ernestine something-or-other, didn't seem to give a damn about what people thought, which I always took as a healthy sign of personal independence.

So they drove back downtown to the Blue Moon Café, where Audie could get his favorite dish on Saturday night. Calf liver and bacon. He'd even taught the cook at the Blue Moon to fix his liver so it was pink when he cut into it, which was another thing the local citizens said marked him as a barbarian, although it has always seemed to me there is no other way to make liver edible.

The Blue Moon had a long counter with a backbar where there was a layout of fresh-made pies and the coffee urns and stacks of hamburger buns still in their wax-paper wrapping. Along the far wall were booths, and down the center of the floor a single row of tables with red-and-white-checked tablecloths. The place always smelled of floor polish and fried onions.

Audie and Ernestine took a booth and gave their order to a waitress who weighed about what Joe Louis did and was wearing one of those pink waitress dresses with a white apron in front that had a few catsup stains on it. She was chewing gum, of course.

Audie lit a Chesterfield cigarette and him and Ernestine were about to shed their overcoats when the other five poker players walked in.

The lead guy was carrying a bat that was all chewed up along the barrel like somebody had been playing pepper with limestone rocks instead of baseballs. The others were making loud noises and knocking over chairs. Rumor had it that one of them paused long enough to throw up in one corner, but that never came out in testimony at the trial.

Some pretty dirty words were passed, sending the waitress running back through the double swinging doors to the kitchen and causing the proprietor behind the cash register up front to drop his *True Detective* magazine. Audie didn't say much, so it was testified, but just looked at these yelling guys with his yellow eyes and a grim little smile on his lips. But his face got a lot pinker.

He decided it was a good time to retreat, so he stood up and threw a handful of five-dollar bills on the table and said, "You fellas have a nice supper on me."

Then him and Ernestine walked out, fast, leaving the five guys yelling insults about Audie's ancestry and sexual inadequacies.

The LaSalle was parallel-parked about twenty steps from the front door of the Blue Moon. Audie opened the door for his lady to get in, then turned and started around the back of the car to get to the driver's side. And right there, coming through the snow toward him, were the five guys, the one out front waving the ball bat and screaming about what a double-barrel son of a bitch Audie Renkin was.

At the trial, Rex Scadins said that if Audie Renkin had walked around the front of the car to get to the driver's side, he'd have got clean away. But he didn't, so there he was, face to face with five guys who were drunk and mad and one with a ball bat and not six steps away from him and bearing down fast.

Audie must have figured he'd retreated far enough. He reached inside his overcoat and hauled out a Smith & Wesson .44 Special revolver and started shooting. Those who were on Main Street that evening said it sounded like Ladyfinger firecrackers, the racket muffled by the still-falling snow.

The guy with the ball bat went down face first, and the other four skidded to a halt and turned and started running back toward the front door of the Blue Moon. Audie kept shooting until all six chambers in the cylinder were empty. And there they were, all five of the poker players sprawled in the snow, blood all over the place as black in the twilight as Aunt Rachel's barbecue sauce.

Then Audie shoved the pistol back inside his coat, walked around the car, and got in. He had a little trouble starting it, but when he did, he drove six blocks down Main Street, pulled into the bus station parking lot, turned the LaSalle over to Ernestine, and, without a kiss or a handshake or even a

good-bye, went into the bus station and bought a ticket for
Muskogee, having decided it was a good time to visit Oklahoma.

Nobody knows, except maybe Audie, why he didn't just
drive away in the LaSalle. But he didn't. He just bought a
ticket on a bus that wasn't even due for forty minutes and
would probably be late at that, what with the snow.

So naturally the Tadmor police found him sitting there in
that drab, toilet-smelling waiting room and arrested him for
disturbing the peace, carrying a concealed weapon, and assault with intent to kill. The serious stuff came later, after the
cops learned that four men were dead, three shot in the back,
and a fifth seriously wounded by a steel-jacketed slug in the
ass, taken as he tried to dive under a car parked in front of
the Blue Moon.

I've heard of some incredible things in my life, but that
twenty-three-year-old kid shooting five guys and then just
sitting there in the bus station not half a dozen blocks from
where the blood was frozen in the snow and caked all over
the Blue Moon floor where they'd dragged the victims is the
height of something or other.

Well, all the details of the shooting came out at the trial.
And me and Emmy Joe cut three full days of classes and
caught holy hell from Mr. Sylvester Longburn, our beloved
high school principal, not to mention a tongue-blistering at
home. Even as big as I was, I thought my mother was going
to run out into the backyard and get a fistful of those little
willow switches she used to stripe my legs with when I'd
really screwed up.

But I'll tell you, that trial was worth it.

The court was packed, like it always was for the frequent
murder trials held there. Like most courthouses in the South,
they had a balcony, and me and Emmy Joe managed to
squeeze in at the rail, where we could look right down on
things. The judge was behind this big natural oak pulpit and

over along one wall was the jury box and the witness chair
between. There was a table in front of the jury where they laid
out physical evidence, and there was the .44 cannon Audie
had used, introduced by the prosecution, and the splintered
ball bat, introduced by the defense.

Audie sat there beside Rex Scadins at their own little table. He was dressed in a stiff new suit that looked like it cost
about fourteen dollars right off the rack at Montgomery Ward.
There wasn't much expression on his face, except that when
each witness came onto the stand, he watched them with
those wolf eyes of his, like he'd as soon bite their foot as go
to Sunday school. He had a fresh haircut that made his ears
stick out considerable, and they were no small ears to start
with. Sometimes Rex Scadins would whisper to him and Audie would nod, but I never once saw him open his mouth to
say anything. And Rex didn't call him in his own defense,
which Emmy Joe said was a big mistake.

The final arguments were a rehash of what had gone before
and got pretty boring until Rex Scadins finished his spiel and
turned back to the defense table. Then he stopped right in the
middle of the pit and looked at the crowd. Not at the jury,
mind you, but the crowd. And he said something I'll never
forget.

"Well, now, it was pretty dark and he had only six shots
and there were five of them getting ready to attack him. He
had to shoot fast. So we've just got to give him something for
marksmanship, don't we?"

Jesus, I couldn't believe it. It was the kind of remark I
guess had been made in a lot of places and a lot of times before, but I'd never heard it, and this lawyer was talking about
a defendant who had shot four guys *in the back*.

The crowd howled and the jury laughed, too, like it was one
of Jack Benny's best jokes about Fred Allen. Jesus! Even the
jury laughed!

That jury still hangs in my mind. About half of them were
wearing bib overalls. The other half were in shirtsleeves and

one guy had on a bow tie and you could see where his hat came down on his forehead because that's where the sunburn started.

You see, this was a long time before I realized that one of the most important things a defense lawyer does is select the jury to his own advantage. And the twelve men sitting in the box that day looked like they knew about living hardscrabble, about cutting crossties from solid oak to sell to the railroad for a few dollars so that maybe the children could get new caps before fall. Like maybe they knew how it was to have the kids rotate going to school in winter because there were only enough coats for half of them. Like maybe they understood that Audie Renkin knew all about swapping shoes with brothers so at least some of them each day could walk ten miles to learn a little reading and figures while the others stayed home, barefooted.

They had shared his experience of working in a rocky hillside field trying to grow sorghum cane so there could be molasses for the cornbread, and hunting squirrels in the woods behind the house so there'd be a little meat on the table. They must have known that all his life until he came to civilization he had never known there was such a thing as an indoor toilet with running water, but only a two-holer shack by the hog pen where the business had to be done quickly during snowtime or else freeze all the naked parts of him that covered one of those holes as the wind whistled up out of the hickory hollows and through the cracks in the privy.

You had the feeling it was that kind of jury.

When they went out, me and Emmy Joe walked up the street to the Castle Lunch for a bowl of red. Sitting next to us on one of the counter stools was Clarence Stoddard, of the Tadmor Hotel. He gave us a hard look.

"I seen you boys in the balcony when I testified," he said. "You oughta be ashamed, playin' hooky."

"We had notes from home," Emmy Joe said with a big smile.

"Well, I'll tell you boys something," Clarence Stoddard said. "That Audie Renkin's gonna get the electric chair. The first one mighta been self-defense, but then he shot all them others in the back. And they never even asked me what that last hand was he won."

"What was it?" I asked.

"Audie beat three of a kind with a dinky little ole seven-high straight."

Me and Emmy Joe couldn't wait for the jury to come in because it was getting dark. So we hurried home and found notes there from Mr. Sylvester Longburn, the bastard, and we caught hell, like I mentioned. Besides that, I had to force down a big bait of pork and beans and fried potatoes and bacon so my mother wouldn't know I'd spoiled my supper eating chili at the Castle Lunch. I didn't sleep a wink that night, what with all the stuff fermenting in my belly and seeing Audie Renkin's face in my mind and hearing Rex Scadins talk about marksmanship.

The next morning, Emmy Joe caught me as I was going into American history class and grabbed my arm in one of those big hands of his. I never saw him so excited. His stepdaddy, the city attorney, had told him the news at breakfast.

"They did the next best thing to an acquittal," he said. "They gave him life. Hell, in this state that means after seven years he'll be eligible for parole. By God, Shanks, they *did* give him something for marksmanship!"

I didn't hear anything more about Audie Renkin until after the War. It was 1947, I guess. Me and Emmy Joe were in the local college then, him getting ready to be a lawyer and me itching to get the hell out of there and go back in the army.

It wasn't unusual that I hadn't heard of Audie, having been off in the Pacific shooting at Japs. Besides, when a guy went to the state penitentiary prison farm, sometimes *nobody* ever heard of him again.

Anyway, it seems he got his parole and went to Utah and

killed another guy. I don't know the details. While he was waiting trial in some county jail out there, another inmate killed him with a rat-tail file.

"He was looking for it," Emmy Joe said. "Think about it. After the shooting he sat there in that bus station, just waiting to get caught. And when the jury didn't give him the chair, he sat there without a smile or a howdy-do to the jury or to Rex Scadins. Like he was disappointed.

"You know what I think? I think Audie Renkin couldn't help shooting those poor bastards that were crazy enough to push him. Look where he came from! It was all survival and he couldn't afford to be pushed. He couldn't stand it. But then he started getting all that civilization stuffed into him. Driving a truck and making good money and living with a fine-looking woman. So after he'd killed those guys, he couldn't stand that, either. You see?"

"No," I said.

"He was looking for it! He wanted it! He had to have a just punishment for what he'd done, see, and so when that jury didn't give it to him, he went out and found it for himself. He found justice on his own. Like he was finally atoning for his sins."

"Emmy Joe," I said, "you're the craziest son of a bitch I ever knew."

But maybe Emmy Joe was right. I don't know because, like I've said, I never knew much about justice and even less about atoning for sins.

Cecil Renkin left Tadmor right after the trial, I found out. He went over to Oklahoma and became a Pentecostal preacher. I saw him once, not long after the War. He'd come back to Weedy Rough to hold a tent revival meeting. Maybe the last honest-to-God, hog-stomping tent revival in this part of the country.

Cecil had a fine-looking woman for a wife, and about half a dozen kids. The oldest one was named Audie. He had yellow eyes and straight hair cut short and a long face with flat features that looked like they'd been planed from Ozark limestone, and were pretty much the same color except for the pink across his cheeks. He always said "ma'am" and "sir" to his elders.

If you ever see that kid, my advice is don't get into a five-card-stud poker game with him.

Yeah. Maybe Emmy Joe was right about that kid's uncle. Maybe Audie Renkin wanted to get caught. Maybe he wanted to get punished.

I still can't get it out of my mind, and that trial was forty years ago. It's a lot like the words Billie Holiday sang: "Good morning, heartache."

When I was stationed at Fort Dix after the War, I heard her once. Jesus!

Well, Audie Renkin and Billie Holiday, there's a comparison for you. Audie sure wasn't a dope addict. I doubt he even knew what heroin was, yet the way he acted had the same kind of haunted despair and defeat that Lady Day put into every blues song she ever sang.

"Good morning, heartache!"

I drove out into the hills last year, wanting to see the old Renkin place, the place where Audie had started. Like maybe if I could stand on the ground he had stood on, there'd be some answers.

But I couldn't even find it. The house is gone, fallen down and stripped by passersby, I guess. So all along that stretch of dirt road in the hills there's nothing but jack oak and sassafras and persimmon where rocky fields once were, and where there used to be a yard where the Renkin kids played.

Well, maybe they didn't get to play much.

Anyway, there weren't any answers. It's all gone. I guess it's been gone for a long time.

7

Knights of
the Flaming Circle

Shanks Caulder's home country wasn't Deep South. People he grew up with in those hills didn't think or talk or act like cotton-culture folk.

And it wasn't Southwest, either. Nobody Shanks knew in those early years owned a cattle ranch or an oil well. The first armadillo didn't migrate into his hills until well after Shanks had completed an army career and come home to stay.

It was just white oak and limestone country, where flat surfaces of any considerable size were rare, and where citizens didn't get so set in their ways with hidebound opinions the way some people did, partly because they hadn't really seen many people who were different from themselves and so had little experience in developing hatreds and fears of other groups.

Oh, they could hate as well as anybody, but usually it was scatter-shooting. When they threw a little hook or two into somebody just because that somebody was a Catholic or was born in New Jersey or wore an orange-colored shirt in the week before the Texas game, there was little real viciousness in it, and usually not even much heat.

As much as any people anywhere, they'd come to under-

stand the old saying "Live and let live." And maybe some of that was because as likely as not they sat each Sunday in church beside some son of a bitch who was the same color as they were and spoke the language as incoherently and ate the same kind of chicken-fried steak once a week and to them was crazy as hell and with a mean streak besides, but who had the same problem putting meat on the table and clothes on his kids' backs and despised unions and Yankees and garlic in his gravy.

So trying to figure out how every grain of sand on the beach of humankind was a bit different from all the other grains just simply took too much effort. So each went about his own business without expending the effort required to really know his brethren, and he expected everybody else to do the same damned thing.

First, let me tell you that the statute of limitations has run out on anything we ever did. And second, because all the other guys who were a part of it are dead, there's no harm in telling about the Knights of the Flaming Circle.

It was the kind of thing boys got wrapped up in before the War and before they'd really come to grips with what bothered them most. Girls. Matter of fact, the War mostly brought on the possibilities of girls to us all. That was when we got out of town to other places—big places, like cities—where we

135

didn't have to worry about friends and family all thinking, like our preachers, that any little bit of girl-and-boy stuff would send us straight to hell.

In a small town, serious girl-and-boy stuff could bring the smell of brimstone. So there was this bottled-up juice that could only come out when we got away, and the War got us away. In those big cities, as far as I can tell, and even in places like Killeen, Texas, which is cheek-by-jowl with Fort Hood, no disrespect intended toward Killeen ladyhood, everybody made out pretty well.

At least, the ones who lived long enough.

The Knights of the Flaming Circle was in a time before the War, when folks were more interested in the next moving-picture show coming to the Palace Theater than in what was happening in Manchuria. Well, I guess by then the Japs had started calling it Manchukuo.

And if I offend anybody by calling them Japs, well, that's what we called them, even before they bombed Pearl Harbor. If somebody's offended, it's just tough titty.

Besides, the Japs don't have anything to do with any of this and I'm sorry I brought it up.

The place to start is with Emmy Joe Gorman. He was one smart guy. But somehow, him and me hit it off even though he was two grades ahead of me in the county seat high school. We used to sit on the corner of Main and Gladstone in front of the Baptist church, and talk late at night, sometimes as late as ten o'clock. There wasn't any traffic there then. It would be quiet and still and the stars would be shining and we'd wonder how many of them had burned out six billion years ago but were so far away that the light was still coming to us. Things like that.

There's a bank of electric traffic signals on that corner now, and any pedestrian trying to cross the intersection even as late as two A.M. takes his life in his hands. And any street-wise dog won't go near the place.

Every time I pass that intersection, I think of the times me and Emmy Joe sat there in the dark and talked. The old church back then was sandstone, with a high dome. Now it's mostly chrome and glass and white brick that turns color when it rains. It looks more like a stockbroker's office than a church.

Emmy Joe wasn't a very big guy, except for his head, which held all those brains, and his hands, which did all those sleight-of-hand tricks. I was always a good seven or eight inches taller than he was and, I thought, a helluva lot more handsome. But there was something about him, missing in me, that attracted the girls. Smooth talk more than anything else, I guess. And a manner that made you think he'd just arrived from Paris, France. I suppose Emmy Joe knew more about girls when he was in high school than I know now.

He walked with a kind of slump to his shoulders, his straight hair hanging down across his forehead, his brown eyes darting around to take in everything, and there always seemed to be a headlong purpose to his walking, like he was headed for something important that nobody else knew anything about. Even when he was standing still, he looked as though he was about ready to launch off in some new direction.

One of my claims to fame is that as time went along I was about the only guy around that Emmy Joe would sit still for and talk. With everybody else, he was like a coiled spring. I always counted that as a big measure of his vast intellect.

Emmy Joe went on in later days to become a linguist. He spoke Spanish and German. He collected fine art. He was a helluva writer, better than I ever would have been. He became the best damned criminal lawyer in this part of the country. And last year he died. My world hasn't been the same since. Sometimes, years after the Knights of the Flaming Circle were forgotten, we didn't see each other very often, but he was always in a special corner of my thinking. A place reserved for knights and heroes and bigger-than-life sons of bitches. I think he felt the same way about me.

Emmy Joe decided we needed an organization to represent chivalry and to protect womanhood. He said we had the lances for the job. All it took was learning to use them.

That's how he described it to us—a little club that stood for justice and right and democracy and the flag. Equal parts to the Stars and Stripes and the old Confederate Stars and Bars of General Lee. Jesus, the way those old Stars and Bars have been prostituted. Now guys drive around in pickup trucks with a decal of it on the front bumper and it means "We hate niggers." When me and Emmy Joe were growing up, it meant courage and sacrifice and facing death every day as a part of the Southern armies. We didn't know much about politics and inequity during the Civil War, but we sure knew a lot about the Rebel army.

Emmy Joe said this would be an outfit against oppression and wrongdoing. None of us knew exactly what any of this meant, except for Emmy Joe maybe. To most of us, oppression meant that our mothers wouldn't let us go to Delano's Eat Shop for ice cream with chocolate syrup on it, even when we had the money in our pockets from selling newspapers or mowing lawns. Wrongdoing meant those evil, dark things in the night that nobody was willing to talk about.

That was as precise as any of us could make it. Except for Emmy Joe, I guess, who never bothered to get into details because he was going to be the Grand Commander. The Grand Commander kept his own counsel, by God, he said, and that was good enough for us.

So Emmy Joe picked his people. Me first. Then the others, all older than me, but I figured if it ever came to a fistfight I could hold my own. Not that it ever did. We were all friends and we felt close together, getting involved in a thing that we knew would give our elders gall bladder trouble or worse if they ever found out.

First there was Jack Horton. Maybe he was picked because his mother lived alone in this old three-story house out on North Main. Most of the place was closed up, and there was a huge basement with a coal furnace. Some Yankee had built it before World War I, and he figured every house needed a furnace. There was a lot of room in the basement spread out around the big toad of a furnace. Concrete floor, too. We could have our meetings there and raise all kinds of hell and nobody would hear us.

Jack was a strange, intense guy. He never had much to do with us or anybody else. He had these black eyes, like an Arab, and a Roman nose, and he moved around like a fox getting ready to inspect the other side of the cage. He never said much.

I guess Jack had to live the rest of his short life with the experience of getting Colette Cloven in the backseat of a 1931 Chevy sedan one night during a football game. As soon as he had his hands on her petticoat, he threw up all over her. He hadn't been drinking or anything like that. He just felt that petticoat and chucked all his cookies onto her nice new dress.

Anyway, Jack's mother's place was a great old house. Back then, North Main was covered over by the limbs of the big elm trees that grew along either side. Like a cathedral. Now, where the old house stood is a Kentucky Fried Chicken place and there isn't a tree in sight for four miles in either direction.

Each time I drive past that Colonel Sanders joint I just look at it and think, "You son of a bitch, you don't even know what you're sitting on."

Then there was Kirk Elander. He was a mite, the smallest of us all and a mad-scientist type. He thought mostly in quadratic equations. He had acne and dandruff and he brushed his teeth only on his birthday. When he was fourteen, he bought a clawhammer to protect himself from people trying to come into his room. It was a no-trespassing area, even for his family.

But I was invited in there a lot of times. It was amazing,

like something out of a bad monster moving-picture show, with beakers and Bunsen burners and coils of colored wire and fruit jars filled with sparkling crystal stuff. In one corner was a two-gallon glass jug. Kirk used this to mix Skim-Blim, which consisted mostly of grain alcohol. He'd stolen the jug from the chemistry department at the local college. Sometimes he called it Purple Passion because along with the grain alcohol it was made with grape juice. Kirk Elander said that any girl who took a swig or two of Purple Passion would do anything. Actually, I never heard of a girl stupid enough even to look at Purple Passion, much less take a swig of it.

Kirk liked to sit around like a Hindu god or something, grinning. He said he knew all the world's questions. Not the answers, just the questions. From the time Kirk Elander was a freshman in high school, I don't think he ever drew a truly sober breath. If you got home late at night and your mother asked you where you'd been, you never admitted having seen Kirk Elander; you'd say, "I been out consorting with lepers," or some other good excuse.

Deke Sanders was a trombone player, like me. He was almost as tall as me but skinny and with a thatch of hair that was like the ruff on a brindle bull in midsummer, stiff and short. His eyes were so bad that without the thick glasses he always wore, he couldn't see the end of his trombone. Deke had these big teeth, kind of horsey, and they seemed to fill out his mouth from one side to the other with no room to spare. His lips were thick and he liked telling the story about the high school band instructor who told him he'd have to play a reed instrument because those lips would never fit into the mouthpiece of a trumpet or an alto horn. And there he was, a fine trombone player. He called it his slush pump.

Deke hummed a lot and never mentioned his daddy, who was a state policeman. We were all grateful to him for that.

And finally, there was Pepper Winnington, red-haired and blue-eyed and always laughing, and all too often getting into fistfights with one of the guys from the south end of town, who usually whipped his butt. But Pepper didn't have a care in the world. He was our free spirit.

Pepper claimed he was the first guy in his class to get the clap. We never knew if it was true. If it was, his folks must have taken him to Tulsa for the cure, because if a doctor in town had done it, we'd surely have heard about it. I can't ever remember Pepper bringing a date to a dance or a Halloween party. He was always the dapper stag, with a bow tie. He'd just flit around among the other stags, giggling and telling stories he'd heard at the Gulf Station Café.

Maybe if he got a dose, it came from rubbing against an infected telephone pole. That's all I could figure. Nobody ever heard of him getting near enough a girl to get it.

Pepper's parents didn't seem to mind his being out late at night. Sometimes he'd wander around town after everything was closed, going from lamppost to lamppost and laughing to himself. Sometimes even in the rain. He was a weird guy.

Looking back, I guess I'd have to say that most of the Knights were weird. But the National Honor Society had asked each of us to join, so you see we made pretty good grades in school. I suppose we were all proud of the little golden pins, but none of us ever admitted it.

So that was it, a very exclusive group.

Well, there was one more. He wasn't a member, but he got involved. His name was J.D. Solomon, a black guy and pretty old by our standards. He wasn't chocolate-colored or tan or sepia. He was black. He lived down in the Canyon, which is what we called the little community on the edge of town where all the colored folks lived. There weren't very many of them. And a few had red hair, for whatever that's worth.

You see, we were hill country, and during slave days there wasn't much market for blacks—no cotton or rice or any other kind of plantation stuff. So there were just a few blacks here and there who groomed horses or were house servants. After the Thirteenth Amendment, not many more came in.

In our day, most of the black men worked as shine boys in

the various barbershops or as bellhops in one of the two hotels or as houseboys in one of the college fraternity houses.
The women worked in the big houses up on Mount Sidney
where the Senator's mother lived. J.D. worked for Jack Horton's mother in the house on North Main.

He was a large one, old J.D. When white mothers with little kids who were misbehaving saw J.D. on the streets, they'd
say, "Look at that big colored man! He'll get you if you don't
hush that whining!"

The kids usually hushed. God, I'm glad my mother never
said anything like that to me.

J.D. had been a boxer, fighting in dim barns and ware-
houses with some other black guy while all the white men
shouted and whooped and bet money on who would beat the
other one to a pulp. His boxing was probably responsible for
his acquiring the small business that he ran in addition to
keeping house for Mrs. Horton. He was a bootlegger.

There was this guy in town named Sheldon Backer. We
called him Tiger because that's what he'd been called when
he was a fighter. He was pretty good, a middleweight. He
knocked out a guy in Kansas City in 1927 and won the Golden
Gloves title or some such thing.

Anyway, Tiger had a liquor store. And he hit it off with J.D.
because they could sit around on slow afternoons and tell lies
about what they'd done in the ring, all the while fingering the
scar tissue over their eyes.

J.D. started using some of his wages from Mrs. Horton to
buy pints of Tiger's merchandise. Then he'd take it to his little house down in the Canyon and hold on to it until some
white guy drove up on Sunday, looking for a bottle. Getting
a bottle on Sunday was hard as hell. So J.D. would sell his
booze at twice what he paid for it, and as far as I hear nobody ever complained.

After a while, J.D. started wholesaling to the black guys
who were bellhops in the hotels. Everybody made a tidy

profit, because Tiger sold his stuff to J.D. at cost, seeing as how they were both old box fighters. Before long, J.D. had a good business. He stayed on with Mrs. Horton because he figured she could never find anybody else. At the time of the Knights of the Flaming Circle, he was driving a 1931 Cadillac four-door, blood-red and with a cut-out on the muffler so he could roar through the Canyon with the thing wide open, sounding like seven freight-train locomotives, and all the black ladies would run out on their porches and wave.

Hell, a lot of times he stopped, too. Just to visit.

J.D. never married. But I suppose he had maybe seventeen kids down there in the Canyon. It was that kind of Cadillac.

But old J.D. was part of the town, you see. Like he'd always been there, him and his car with a trunkful of Tiger Backer's bonded whiskey, and during a time that the state wouldn't have licensed him to sell booze or beer even if his uncle had been George Washington Carver.

J.D. never drove the red Cadillac to work at Mrs. Horton's. He always walked. He figured it wouldn't look right, him pulling into a driveway with that big car, into a driveway where there hadn't been an automobile since the Crash of '29.

Man, oh man, the seasons when I was a kid!

In winter sometimes an ice storm would come and sheath every twig in crystal, and when the sun came out to shine on it, the world was so dazzling it hurt your eyes. Every kid in town had a sled, but only got to use it about once a year, because it didn't snow all that much. But when it did, we'd all go to Spring Street and ride the steep incline all the way to Main, toes frozen and noses red and thinking about afterward when we'd go home and have a cup of hot spiced tea and a big chunk of gingerbread.

Then the spring. My God, you've never seen anything like the spring. A jungle popping out green everywhere and the locust trees like lettuce and the dogwood blossoms like

snowballs and the redbud like bouquets of lilac in a sweet lady's hand. You couldn't walk down a single street without
smelling the honeysuckle.

And summer. Well, summer could get pretty hot. But there
were always plenty of swimming holes within walking distance, and they opened the city park pool in 1934, a WPA
project. But even summer had its moments, with cool breezes
in the evening, and you would sit on the front-porch swing
and watch the cardinals in the wild cherry trees and sometimes late goldfinches, up from Central America, so our bi-
ology teacher said, flitting around like little pats of butter in
the lowering sunlight. And summer was lemonade time.

Best of all was fall. The gum trees would go blood-red and
the maples flaming orange and the sycamores and elms as
golden as the stuff they keep at Fort Knox. And the scent of
leaves burning in the gutters was everywhere. I could never
understand how anything that smelled as good as burning
leaves could pollute the air. They've got ordinances now
against burning leaves, and all the elms are gone. Only a few
maples are left, and no walnuts because they were all cut
down to make furniture and gun stocks.

There are still a lot of tough old oaks around. I remember
one out on Telegraph Road with a trunk so big that three of
us with arms extended couldn't reach around it. Some guy at
the college last year said it was probably three hundred years
old. That was two centuries before the Cherokees came into
this country, which is something to think about. In the au-
tumn its leaves turn to rusty brown, the kind of rusty brown
that glints in the sun like metal.

That's how it looked when Emmy Joe called the first meeting of the Knights of the Flaming Circle in the basement of
Jack Horton's mother's house on North Main.

Everything was very serious. Emmy Joe stood at the head
of this long table and we sat around it on old nail kegs that
had been left over from the time the house was built before

World War I by that Yankee. There was a fire in the furnace, and some light flickered out through the slotted feed door. On the table, just in front of Emmy Joe, was a wine bottle with a candle stuck in it, and the flame cast shivering yellow lights across Emmy Joe's face.

The wine bottle was empty, of course, and the label had a lot of French words on it. We figured he'd gotten it from the trash bin at home. His stepfather was city attorney and a well-educated man, and liked to drink wine from France and beer from Germany and vodka from Finland and things like that, any one bottle of which cost almost as much as my mother paid for rent on our house for a month.

So it was all very impressive.

But also spooky.

What little light there was didn't begin to penetrate to the far corners of that big dark basement. The orange flame of the candle caused little ghostlike dancings among the cobwebs overhead. Outside, there was a wind making strange noises in the old dry leaves of the three hickory trees there, and the same wind made a sighing sound under the eaves and through a crack in one of the basement windowpanes. And right at the center of it all was Emmy Joe's face like a skull, his brown eyes shining and the hair falling over a dome of bone-white forehead.

I don't know about the others, but the whole business made goose bumps all along my arms.

First, Emmy Joe made a speech about honor. I don't recall the words, but they must have been first-rate because even Pepper Winnington was listening with his mouth open. Then Emmy Joe took out a little penknife with a sharp point on the blade and pricked the end of his right forefinger. I remember he said that the right forefinger was the locus of power for all knights. Whatever that meant. It was fine with us.

Then he went around the table and pricked each of us on the right forefinger and it hurt like hell. With Emmy Joe in-

structing, we passed among one another, pressing our bleeding fingers together. So Emmy Joe said we were all brothers
in blood and could never tell the secrets of the Knights of the
Flaming Circle on pain of horrible death. Then he read a passage about courage and devotion to duty from *All Quiet on
the Western Front*, where this infantry company comes back
from the line with only twenty-seven guys left.

We sat there and watched as Emmy Joe went back behind
the furnace and came out with a little hoop made from a metal
coat hanger and with straw tied on all around, and from the
smell we knew it had been soaked in gasoline. He held it over
the candle and the circle leaped into flame and he yelled, "For
Camelot!"

Whatever that meant.

Then he took a little bottle of Skim-Blim, after the circle
had burned out, and we knew he'd got that from Kirk Elander. He passed it around and each one of us took a sip, and
after each sip Emmy Joe said, "Excalibur, the sword of
truth."

So after that, Emmy Joe brought out some more bottles and
put candles in them and lit them and produced a deck of cards
and said that at the next meeting we'd decide on our mis-
sions, and we spent an hour or two playing penny-ante poker.
Nobody's mind was really on poker, I guess. I won twenty-
seven cents.

Emmy Joe said we needed some uniforms. Whoever heard
of knights without some kind of uniform? he said. Chain mail
and armor was too heavy, he said, and besides that, there
wasn't much of that kind of thing available in northern Arkansas. But he had something just as good. And he knew
where to find it.

We all figured afterward that it was because his stepdaddy
was city attorney and Emmy Joe had heard stuff around the
house when the grownups were having cocktails or some such
thing. A guy never knows what good stuff he can pick up if

he just stands around and listens to grownups when they're having cocktails.

Now, we didn't consider ourselves kids, you see. We were all at least sixteen. But we still called people older than twenty-five grownups.

Anyway.

At the second meeting of the Knights, Emmy Joe selected his death squad. That's what he called it. A death squad. He'd lead it, of course, and he chose me because I was the tallest. He chose Kirk Elander because he was the smallest. We didn't understand at the time why the tallest and the smallest had any importance.

We left the others in the basement playing blackjack under that wine-bottle candle, and went out into the night. I guess it was about nine o'clock.

We were hardly out onto the sidewalk in front of the house and moving toward town when Emmy Joe told us. He'd really chosen me and Kirk because he reckoned we were the most reliable when there was danger. Kirk Elander snickered as though he figured Emmy Joe was just blowing smoke, but it made me feel pretty good. You take what you can get in this life. Hearing Emmy Joe say something about danger raised a few goose bumps along my arms.

It was six blocks to the town square. That's where we headed, Emmy Joe in front, walking with that bent-forward intensity, and me and Kirk hurrying along behind and nobody saying anything. We walked to the northwest corner of the square and found a dark spot alongside the wall of the Federal Bank Building.

Across the street was the Claxon Building. The Claxons had been selling insurance for as long as anyone could remember, and now they owned the biggest building in town, four stories. The night Emmy Joe and me and Kirk Elander stood there looking at it, the top two floors were empty. Those were Depression days, and renting office space wasn't easy, especially as in those days there weren't two lawyers for every citizen.

On the second floor were the insurance offices. On the first was the city administration. The city was as poor as everybody else and didn't own much, so they rented the space they needed. There was a single staircase that led from the sidewalk up about a half-dozen steps to the first-floor hallway. The first door on the left along that hallway, visible from the street, was half glass and it showed a light inside. Printed across the glass was one word, in black letters: POLICE.

Well, by then Kirk and me knew we had come to steal something, and right under the noses of the city police. Our city policemen weren't much, but they all carried .45 pistols. And in those days policemen shot first and asked questions later. I don't know about Kirk Elander, but as soon as the thing hit home I was ready to get the hell out of there. But I remembered what Emmy Joe had said about reliability, and I stayed.

Emmy Joe started whispering.

"All the city cops are in there playing pitch, all three of them," he said. "So when we go past the door we've got to be very quiet. We'll crawl by under the glass."

Emmy Joe and me and Kirk knew the cops were all in there because the 1935 Ford sedan squad car was sitting at the curb. It had a siren on one front fender, looking like a stack of metallic waffles. On the other front fender was a red-globed chrome light that looked like a naval shell.

"Before we start, let's let the air out of the tires," Kirk snickered.

"Hell, no," Emmy Joe said, like a snake hissing. "Those three guys could run us down on foot if we get caught. The thing is, we're not going to get caught!"

Those steps leading into the hall were concrete, so there wasn't any creaking. As we slithered under the lighted door window we could hear the cops inside making bids in their

pitch game. There was a radio, too. The best I recall, it was
Fred Allen and Portland exchanging gags. Then we were into
the hall and headed for the stairway to the upper floors and
when we put a foot on them the damned boards sounded like
mules braying.

Every inch of the way I was expecting those guys to run
out and start spraying the whole place with .45 slugs. But I
guess their game was pretty intense or else Fred Allen was
making some good jokes. I always liked Fred Allen ever
since.

We went up to the second floor in the dark, and then Emmy
Joe produced a small flashlight. We went on up to the third
floor, fast, Kirk Elander giggling all the way. Here I was in a
cold sweat, and that son of a bitch liked it.

On the top floor, Emmy Joe put his light on the doors.
When we came to 403, we stopped and Emmy Joe pulled a
screwdriver from under his shirt. I don't know where he carried that stuff, the flashlight and the screwdriver, but he had
them.

"Up on Shanks's shoulders," he whispered to Kirk Elander.

This was one of those old doors with a hinged glass tran-
som at the top. Kirk shinnied up on my shoulders to pry it
open with the screwdriver. He wasn't very heavy, but all my
senses were in high gear. I could smell the musty odor of old
lofts, long unoccupied. I could feel the grain of the wood in
that door with the tip of my nose as I held Kirk on my shoulders. I could hear the clock in the courthouse tower striking
ten like it was right at the end of the hall. I could hear the
click of metal as the cops rolled back the hammers of their
.45s.

"We got it," Emmy Joe whispered, and suddenly the
weight of Kirk Elander was off my shoulders and I heard him
cursing. Inside the door.

"I tore my goddamn pants," he said.

Then the door opened and there was Kirk Elander, grinning in the shine of Emmy Joe's light.

"Come on," Emmy Joe said.

I'd never seen anything like it. There were all these packing crates, yellow pine and clean and smelling like they just came from the lumberyard. Emmy Joe took the screwdriver from Kirk Elander and opened the first one, a big one, holding the flashlight in one hand as he pried off the top with the screwdriver.

"Jesus!" Kirk said, and he wasn't giggling now.

There were all these white robes, clean as heaven and lined with silk, red and yellow and purple and orange, and these little emblems on the fronts with crosses and wings and devil's faces and everything smelling like mothballs. And for each robe, a pointy hood.

"Grab a handful," Emmy Joe said, and we did.

I don't even remember getting out of there. I think we left the door open. We went down the stairs and crawled past that police door carrying the robes, and inside we could still hear Fred Allen laughing it up. We were out into the street then, and I almost died because Kirk Elander, his arms full of white cloth, paused a minute beside the police car like he wanted to let the air out of the tires. Jesus!

We slipped along alleys going back, like John Dillinger after a big bank job. My heart was about to jump right through my ribs. And then finally we were back in Mrs. Horton's basement, and I never thought an old dusty furnace could look so good. We dumped the stuff in the middle of the table, right in the middle of all the cards and the pennies.

"Where the hell you guys been?" Pepper Winnington asked.

"Oh, my God," Deke Sanders said. "We've robbed the Klan!"

"We sure as hell have!" Kirk shouted, and started grabbing those robes and throwing them up in the air and then holding a wad of them close to his belly and dancing around the table.

"The meeting's adjourned," Emmy Joe said. "Fold up those uniforms and we'll put 'em in the corner, and in time we'll decide the next step."

I've thought about that night a lot in the intervening years, and come to the conclusion that throughout history the times of greatest heroes are also the times of greatest scoundrels. And sometimes they are one and the same.

In our part of the country the Klan had never amounted to much more than a social club. Usually on the Fourth of July they'd hold a big public barbecue at the fairgrounds and all the members would show up in their robes and sweat through the ninety-degree heat. According to historians, who are supposed to know about such things, this particular bunch never burned a single cross in the Canyon, or anywhere else, and there sure as hell had never been a lynching.

They tried to keep their membership secret, but it wasn't any big deal.

All my life I'd heard that we had a bunch of nice colored folks in our town. They knew their place, people said, and didn't come wandering around in the main residential areas after dark. All the kids I knew had always been taught not to say "nigger." And every family in town that could afford it had a black family or two they could call on if a drain needed fixing or trees needed pruning or kids needed watching while a new one was about to be born. When we were young, we always called the adult blacks Uncle or Aunt. It was a peaceful arrangement.

That's what made it all so strange. It showed me for the first time that things can get terribly convoluted and twisted when fake passion of some sort is whipped up. Too often the fake turns to real because some people can hypnotize themselves into believing anything.

The first mission the Knights of the Flaming Circle set for

themselves was to go down into the Canyon one night, wearing the Klan robes and hoods, and march back and forth chanting various ominous things and carrying flaming hoops. Kirk Elander said he could fashion these hoops with coat hangers wrapped in heavy cotton cloth, soaked in coal oil that would burn for twenty minutes.

During the night that decision was made, Emmy Joe didn't say much. He watched the others, and I watched him. It was like he was saying to himself, "Jesus, what have I started here?" He just let it roll as though he was fascinated with seeing where it would all lead.

"We'll show 'em we haven't forgotten," Kirk said.

"Keep 'em in their place," said Pepper Winnington.

"We'll be protecting the white womanhood of this fair city," Deke Sanders said.

I almost laughed at that one. In all my life, I'd never heard of a female in town being afraid of anybody from the Canyon.

Anyway, it was decided by vote, me and Emmy Joe abstaining, so we got out the robes and hoods and everybody got one. Mine was nice. A red silk lining and a gold cross on the left breast. The hood was a little too big for my head, and the thing kept slipping down so I couldn't see through the eye slits in the front.

We marched around the table in the candlelight, singing "Pretty Polly." Now this was a very lewd song all about crawling and creeping up to the bedroom where Polly was sleeping on a night of lightning and thunder. I never was able to figure out what it had to do with the Knights of the Flaming Circle, except maybe it was our version of rebelling against elders who would have turned pea-green if they'd ever heard the words of that tune.

Now and then, between verses and when everybody else was taking a deep breath, Emmy Joe shouted, "Excalibur, sword of truth!" He was leading the parade like a drum major, with his hood pulled back off his face so he could see.

Then we sat down around the table and started working out the logistics. We'd get to the Canyon by walking, of course. We could all drive, except maybe for Kirk Elander, but nobody had his own car and wouldn't dare ask for the family one for such a venture.

"How do we get out after our little stint?" asked Jack Horton. It was the first thing he'd said for a long time, just sitting there looking like a fox.

Well, we'd have to come out like we went in, on foot, said Emmy Joe. Then, showing his leadership, he took out some paper and a pencil. I never knew Emmy Joe not to have some paper and a pencil handy. He drew a street map of the town around the Canyon. And he and Deke Sanders got into one hell of an argument about how the streets were situated, but they finally worked it out.

Then Emmy Joe drew a route into the Canyon, and then he drew all these little squiggles. That was how we'd get out, each one running for his life and on his own if those people down there realized we were just a bunch of kids without shotguns.

Everybody sat around the table without saying anything. Coming out in a lot of different directions was fine to confuse the pursuit, as Emmy Joe had said. But being all alone in the night, trying to run for our lives in those goddamned Klan robes, put a new perspective on the thing.

"All right," Emmy Joe said, sensing the tenor of the silence. "We'll all come out together, in a bunch."

"Good," said Pepper Winnington. "We better take some ax handles, just in case."

It was at that moment J.D. Solomon came in, from the outside basement door. He had a bottle of pink-colored wine in one hand and a smile on his face that showed a lot of white teeth. He just walked right in, and we sat there around that table in those Klan robes with our mouths open, looking at the massive black muscles below his rolled-up shirtsleeves, and his knuckles on both fists that we knew were as hard as my grandmother's cast-iron skillet.

"Well, I see you young gentlemans havin' another meetin'," J.D. said, and he walked over to the table and pulled up an empty nail keg and sat down between Emmy Joe and Jack Horton.

Nobody moved. Nobody even breathed. I watched those big black hands with the pink palms as J.D. placed the wine bottle on the table, his movements like liquid music.

"Mr. Jack, I got that leg back on your mama's china closet," J.D. said, looking at Jack. Emmy Joe was the only one of us with his hood off so you could see his face, but J.D. knew us, all right. "I hope I didn't keep her up past her bedtime. Was fixin' to go on home and seen your light and reckoned you might like a little sip of my wine."

"Thank you," said Emmy Joe.

That's when we all started pulling off our hoods. Slow, like it was painful to have the candlelight shine on our faces. We didn't look at J.D.'s eyes. Just his hands. He was working the cork out of the bottle, smiling as though he spent every night of his life in social discourse with a bunch of guys sitting around in Klan robes.

"Have a sip, Mr. Emmy Joe," he said.

"Thank you," said Emmy Joe and took the bottle and tipped it up quickly, then back down.

"You too, Mr. Shanks," J.D. said, pushing the bottle across the table to me. "All you young gentlemans have a little sip, then ole J.D. gone home."

The bottle passed around the table pretty fast and nobody said a word. Except for Emmy Joe. He kept saying "Thank you, thank you."

J.D. took a sip himself and then looked around at us. His eyes stopped on each face and his teeth gleamed.

"Well, gotta go. Mr. Jack, you young gentlemans don't

make too much noise now and keep your mama away from her sleep."

And he was up and gone. I never saw anyone move so fast and so quiet, like quicksilver. One minute he was there, the next minute he was gone.

Me and Emmy Joe looked at each other. Everybody else was looking at us. Then, almost together, me and Emmy Joe jumped up and pulled off our robes and started for the door.

"Where you guys goin'?" Deke asked.

Me and Emmy Joe didn't say anything. We just went.

We caught up to J.D. about two blocks short of the Baptist church. He heard us coming and stopped and turned to wait for us.

"Me and Shanks were going home, too," Emmy Joe said. "Thought we'd walk a ways with you."

"That's fine," J.D. said. "Wanta fresh sip?"

"No, thanks," said Emmy Joe. "Gotta go home and study for a test."

J.D. laughed, a great booming sound that echoed under the spreading branches of the elms.

"Why, Mr. Emmy Joe, you ain't ever had to do no studyin' in your life."

We didn't say much as we walked. Just about the weather and the mockingbirds, and things like that. J.D. walked in the middle and I got the feeling he had shortened his stride to keep from getting ahead of me and Emmy Joe.

At the Baptist church we stopped and Emmy Joe said me and him turned off here. J.D. took a sip of his wine and smacked his lips and offered it to us again but we both said no thanks.

"Funny thing happened," J.D. said. "They was this man come to the Canyon yesterday. Big ole black man, meanlookin' nigger. Just after dark las' night I drove him south on the highway to the railroad junction. Me and some of the other boys said to him they was a freight train about midnight. Maybe he orta get on it. Maybe it'd be nice if he seen some of Texas. This man said he was from Detroit, so we says maybe he ought to go see Texas.

"He wasn't our kinda folks, you know? Come in with all them foreign ideas in his head. Messin' things up. So we allowed to him that he orta go see Texas and not come back aroun' here."

J.D. took another swig and laughed again, only gently this time, like a gurgle in a bathtub drain.

"Gotta watch for things gettin' messed up. But now, Mr. Emmy Joe, don't you go tellin' your daddy about that. He might come down to the Canyon and arrest me for runnin' people out of town. I don't want no city prosecutor on me."

And he laughed some more.

"Well, I'll see you young gentlemans."

And he was walking away along Main, toward the Canyon, and we could see his big black bulk, blacker than the night around him, going away and now and then looking like he was covered with snow as he passed under a streetlight. We waited until he'd gone past three streetlights. Then me and Emmy Joe looked at one another for just a second and turned and started back out North Main. We walked fast and didn't say a word.

The other guys were gone when we got back to Jack Horton's mother's house. They'd left the candle burning in the empty bottle on the table, and there was still a lot of fire in the furnace. We still didn't say anything. We just gathered up all those nice white Klan robes with the red and yellow and purple silk linings. I yanked open the furnace door and Emmy Joe threw the whole lot into the fire.

All the rest of our lives, me and Emmy Joe said we were just getting rid of the evidence because breaking and entering and theft carried a heavy load on conviction. But we burned those robes for a lot more reasons than that. I was never able to figure it out exactly, and I don't think Emmy Joe ever did, either.

Afterward, the bunch got together a couple more times in the basement of Jack Horton's mother's house. We played penny-ante poker by candlelight, but nobody ever mentioned the Knights of the Flaming Circle. The whole thing ceased abruptly after the night Kirk Elander and Deke Sanders got into a helluva fistfight over whether a flush beat a full house.

The War broke the gang up even more, like it did everything else. Oh, there are a lot of stories I could tell about each one of those guys before the War started for us, but we were never together again as a group.

Kirk Elander died right after the bomb dropped on Hiroshima. There wasn't anything in the newspaper about causes. We all figured his insides had rotted out. Deke Sanders was run over by a fire truck in Muskogee, Oklahoma, one night, about 1952. He probably got drunk and lost his glasses and never even saw the truck coming.

Pepper Winnington died in an insane asylum in Birmingham, Alabama, the year after that. But Jack Horton was everybody's pride. He went into the FBI and chased bad guys all over the country, I guess. Right after his mother died during General Eisenhower's second administration, Jack was in a Topeka hotel when he put a .357 Magnum pistol to his forehead and pulled the trigger.

Emerick Joseph Gorman suffered a fatal stroke when he was sixty-one. It rained like hell at the funeral. Everything was dismal, which was just right with the way I felt. Hell, I figured me and Emmy Joe would live forever.

Afterward, I went down to the Canyon to visit J.D. Solomon. I been down there a few times, to his place.

The state liquor board had given J.D. a license to open a little beer joint. He kept a clean saloon and no trouble because he knew if there was any, that license would be yanked fast. He opened about ten each morning and was locked up by seven in the evening.

That rainy day I walked in there, it was loaded with black people, a lot of young ones I didn't know. As soon as I showed up, all talking stopped and every eye in the place was on me like maybe I was a cop come to put the arm on somebody.

Then from the back, J.D. Solomon saw me and yelled loud enough to shake the beer bottles.

"Hey, Shanks!"

Listen, when guys like me, who knew him well, came into J.D.'s place, all that "mister" shit was forgotten.

We went to J.D.'s personal booth in back, where he and his guests could drink any damned thing they wanted, not just the 3.2 beer the state had licensed him to sell. So we sat there and one of his gloriously black good-looking waitresses, who was probably one of his daughters, brought us two bottles of cold Falstaff and two shot glasses and a fifth of Johnnie Black. Me and J.D. had our first boiler-maker with that high-priced Scotch without saying anything.

"I just come from the funeral," I said.

"Yeah, I knew they was buryin' him today," said J.D.

It was hard then not to notice that J.D.'s eyes weren't so bright anymore. And he had lines in his face. And little corkscrew white hairs in his topknot. But at least his teeth were still as strong as a tiger's when he smiled at me.

"There was one helluva crowd," I said.

"Yeah, I reckoned there would be. I'd like to gone."

"Hell, you could have gone with me."

"No," he said, and poured another jolt into our glasses. "It's better people like me remember him out of sight. So here's to a good man."

And then that big son of a bitch, knowing what Emmy Joe had meant to me, reached across the table and patted my hand. I got the hell out of there before I broke down and bawled.

They were having a kind of wake for Emmy Joe in one of the hotel bars. I went, and there were all these judges and lawyers and bankers and I stood in one corner getting a little drunk and looking at them and feeling very alone.

It came to me that something had driven Emmy Joe.
Something had haunted him, maybe. I couldn't say if he was
ever really happy. It seemed he was always looking for whatever it was the Knights of the Flaming Circle stood for, and
never found it. As though he couldn't explain it any better to
himself than he could to the rest of us.

Standing there being jostled by the three-piece-suit crowd
in the hotel bar after we put Emmy Joe down, I sort of wanted
to go back to the Canyon and have a few more jolts with J.D.
Solomon. I think Emmy Joe would have understood that.

8

The Trombone and the Lady

Music has always been a large part of Shanks's life. You might take him for a country-and-western man, but not so. He enjoys that sort of mayhem and a little bluegrass banjo-plucking now and again, but after he came to the county seat when he was about twelve years old, the thing that caught him was big-band swing and jazz. Along with friends who had the same tastes, Shanks spent a lot of time listening to the Dorsey brothers and Benny Goodman and Duke Ellington and Louis Armstrong.

He never had the chance to hear any of these people in person until after the army started running him all over the nation. But in his high school days, he heard them on those old wax-based record discs that could be shattered with a hard look and would warp if left in the sun.

The county seat had a music store called Steinringer's, and there were little glass booths where a person could take a record and listen, the idea being that if you liked it, you'd buy it. Outside, at the entrance, there was a mosaic tile floor in blue and white. Nobody ever paid much attention to it when they walked across it. Now, along with the whole building, it's a National Historic Site, and a place where lawyers dis-

cuss liability, which is a long way from Ruth Etting singing the blues.

Shanks and his friends never bought anything. In fact, Mr. Steinringer had been dead a long time before any of them could afford to buy anything. In those golden days before the War, they just came in to listen and then said "Thank you" to Mr. Steinringer and left until the next day after school, when they'd be back asking for the latest Chick Webb or Charlie Barnet or Sid Catlett platter.

They were never rude or abrupt and they never used bad language in his store, so Mr. Steinringer didn't seem to mind their being in his place. In fact, sometimes he could be found standing just outside the booth, ear cocked to the glass and tapping his foot when the kids inside the little transparent cubicle were wiggling to the throb of Jo Jones on drums or Ben Webster on the tenor saxophone.

It was only a matter of time before Shanks became involved with the high school band. It all depended on how soon he could save enough money from cutting grass to buy an instrument. The kind of instrument didn't matter. So when an old trombone that had likely sounded its first note during the McKinley administration came on the market for seventeen dollars, Shanks bought it. The next semester, he was enrolled in the band.

Of all the things in his life, that trombone provided more adventure and excitement than anything else that ever happened to him. Except, of course, World War II, the police action in Korea, and two tours in Vietnam.

The WPA built the town a rec-
reation hall just south of the county courthouse. It was built
with native sandstone, popular around here with the WPA
because they used the materials at hand. It was ugly as hell.
It looked like a wet cardboard box that had started to develop a little green mold around the edges.

Inside, it wasn't a lot better. There was one long room with
a bandstand at the far end, facing the double doors. On either
side of the bandstand were the rest rooms. POINTERS was lettered on one door and SITTERS on the other, and beneath the

163

words were plywood cutouts of bird dogs. At least they were supposed to be bird dogs. One looked suspiciously like the county judge's bull mastiff.

That WPA architect had enough foresight to make the rest rooms large. There were three stalls for the "sitters" and enough floor space left over for primping before a full-length metal mirror. The "pointers" had two urinals, one stall, and enough room left over for a decent crap game on the concrete floor.

The main ballroom, as they called it, had a concrete floor, too. The WPAers had planed it down pretty good except for a few rough spots the dancers learned to avoid. There was a fifty-five-gallon drum in one corner, with sawdust to sprinkle on the floor. They called that "slicking 'er up." Along both side walls between the windows were white signboards with large red lettering: NO INTOXICATING BEVERAGES ALLOWED.

It might surprise you to know that the warning against booze was taken seriously. Not from any respect for the law, but because everyone knew that if a pint of whiskey or wine jostled out of a hip pocket during a fast fox-trot, there was little chance of survival when it hit that concrete floor.

For musicians on the bandstand, none of the rules applied. They drank straight out of the bottle in front of God and the deputy sheriffs and everybody else. Back then, musicians were set apart, like doctors, because maybe they were the only ones who knew what it was like to get high on pot. Of course, they didn't call it that. They called it gage or Mary Jane.

They didn't call the fun-time cigarettes joints, either. They called them nails or roaches.

Dancers stashed their bottles outside in the weeds, or in the cabs of pickup trucks or sedans. When there was a dance at the rec hall, at any one time you could find half the men and some of the women outside taking a little sip.

There was a single naked light bulb on the outside of the

hall just above the door, suspended on a gooseneck length of pipe. Comers and goers seldom paused in the feeble light because it attracted millions of flying night varmits.

There were the usual drunken fistfights associated with such gatherings, and a few encounters more serious, involving knives. There were a few couplings involving love. A young woman would disappear into the darkness with her man and return in an amazingly short time checking her dress for grass stains, and the guy looking flushed and smug.

Mostly the rec hall stood dark and empty, like a deserted barn. But during the warm months, April through October, once every two weeks Bobby Lew Hillspeth and his Cherokee Playboys came from Tulsa to play a dance on Saturday night. The cover charge was four bits.

Bobby Lew fronted a Western swing band with trumpets and saxes and trombones on the one hand, fiddles and guitars and steel guitars on the other, plus a rhythm section of bass, drums, and piano. They alternated their tunes between hillbilly and popular, so such things as "Huckabee Reel" might be followed by "The Music Goes Round and Round." Then there were polkas and two-steps and an occasional square, but whatever they played, it was loud and fast. And when the steel-guitar man took his chorus, the other musicians would shout, "Take it away, Leon!"

The best dance anyone could remember at the rec hall was sometime in September 1938. It wasn't only a dance but a floor show thrown in, because the band got into a hell of a fight. It happened when the steel-guitar man started a solo on the loomlike contraption he sat behind, and one of the trumpet guys shouted something obscene about weavers. All the string guys tied into all the horn guys and it took the rhythm section and Bobby Lew Hillspeth and three city policemen to restore peace and order.

In between Bobby Lew's appearances, there was this local group that played dances at the rec hall. Aubrey Counts's

Counterpoints. It was a fancy name for another Western swing band with the same setup of instruments as Bobby Lew's. They weren't as professional in their playing, but they were just as loud. The guy who played trombone with them was Deke Sanders, my good buddy who wore thick glasses and had an addictive taste for bourbon whiskey, even in high school. In fact, it was Deke's love of strong drink that gave me my first opportunity to play for money.

In the high school marching and concert band, I played second chair, first stand. That meant I was the number-two guy in the whole trombone section. It didn't happen all at once. It took a while. But I practiced a lot then, during my first years in high school, a routine I later ignored after most of my interest shifted to girls.

There wasn't any chance I'd ever be first chair, because we had this kid named June Kipper. They tell me that back in Civil War times there were a lot of men named June. But in the 1930s you didn't run across very many. So June Kipper took a lot of crap from other students, especially football players, owing to what they called his "pussy" name.

June didn't pay it any mind. He was a smart kid. He had these big blue eyes and fat cheeks and looked like he was already going bald, which he was, and he was only a sophomore.

But, God, he could play trombone! All he did at home was practice. His old man was a doctor at the Veterans' Hospital on North Mountain, just outside of town. He always had money for his kid, this doctor, so June didn't have to spend valuable time throwing newspapers or cutting grass. So he practiced a lot and he could do things on a trombone no kid was supposed to be able to do. We all figured he was the next Jack Teagarden.

None of this seemed to go to June's head. He was just a nice, quiet kid, minding his own business and maybe looking at life through a different set of lenses. He dressed pretty well,

wearing a necktie to school every day, and he had this pair
of suede shoes that knocked me out. They must have cost at
least nine dollars. Ronald Colman was his favorite actor, so
you can see the kind of guy he was. A lot of my friends
thought he was a pansy and wouldn't have anything to do
with him, but man, he wasn't any pansy, as I found out.

I wasn't sure myself, for a long time. But he was still my
friend through all the uncertainty. I always reckoned that to
be the brightest star in my crown, maybe—that no matter
what he was, I was his friend.

Anyway, one of my other friends, Deke Sanders, was
playing his slush pump with Aubrey Counts's band at the rec
hall every odd Saturday night this one summer. I'd never gone
there because it was felt in refined circles that going to the rec
hall for one of those dances was like cracking open the door
to hell. That was in the period when it was important to me
that I be considered refined. Besides, if my mother ever heard
of me going there, she would have whaled the daylights out
of me, even though I was already a head taller than her.

One Friday at the end of a spring semester, right after sixth-
period band practice, June Kipper came up to me and said he
was going to the rec hall that night to hear Aubrey Counts's
band play and would I like to go.

"Hell, June," I said. "You can get your guts cut out down
there."

"I been there a lot," he said. "I been going there a lot."

So I said it was all right with me, if I could convince my
mother I was going to the Smoke Shop to get a cherry shake
and a grilled-cheese sandwich and then just jaw with the guys
while we walked around the square, window-shopping and
looking for girls. Well, I wouldn't tell her the girls part. And
then maybe I'd say we were going to take in a movie at the
Palace, which that weekend was Buck Jones in *Cattle Trail
to Montana* or some such thing.

It made me feel good. Here this guy was, asking me to go

hear some music, and me the one trying to do him out of his first chair in the band. Small chance.

The best part was we could listen to Deke play, and he was older than us and played even better than June.

"Can you get some cigarettes?" June asked.

"Sure," I said. I knew he didn't have the guts to go into a place and ask for a deck of Luckys or anything because he was afraid the guy behind the counter would turn him down because he was so young. Hell, I never had that problem and neither did any of the guys behind the counters.

I never saw anything like it. That was a long time before I understood the mystique of beer joints and highway honky-tonks. It smelled like sweat and sawdust and the noise was enough to hurt your ears and people were swirling around all over the place and yelling at one another and the guys in the band kept shouting, "Take it away, Leon." That's what the musicians in Bobby Lew's band did, so Aubrey Counts's guys did it too, whether they had a guitar man named Leon or not. The whole thing reminded me of a scene out of a movie I saw later called *Fantasia*. Only with a lot more sharp edges.

Every guy I saw on the dance floor or standing around the walls watching the women looked like he could hit a bull in the face with his fist and the bull would go down. The women looked just as tough, but some of them were pretty in a hickory-hard sort of way.

One of those was named Ruthie Scalese. She was the same age as me and June, I found out, and she came to these affairs with her daddy, Antonio Scalese, who was a grape grower from up around Tadmor. Old Tony, as they called him, was a mean-looking guy with arms like crossties and a face that always needed shaving, and more hair in his eyebrows than most people grow on their topknots. Black as midnight, that hair, and black eyes, too, and when you looked at him you could almost smell the tomato sauce he had on his pasta for supper that night.

Ruthie was only one of six daughters in the Scalese family, all of them big-eyed, good-looking, and with Sicilian black hair done up in buns at the napes of their long necks. And you knew just by looking at them that when the pins came out, raven hair would fall all the way to their fantastic butts. But not many guys spent any time looking at them, because Old Tony had one helluva temper and guarded them like a barbed-wire fence.

Everybody figured Tony brought his daughters to the dances at the rec hall so he could keep his eye on them. They always stood in one corner, making their black eyes light up the place, but none of the guys had nerve enough to go over and ask them to dance. So they just stood there, watching their daddy and mama trip the light fantastic on the WPA's concrete floor. Of course, Tony Scalese looked more like a bull elephant in rut than any tripper of lights fantastic.

June Kipper and me stood down in front at the bandstand, listening to Deke play the trombone. They'd built the band-stand about six feet above the level of the dancing surface so the fistfights that broke out among the two-steppers wouldn't spill over into the musicians' domain and dent a lot of instruments. Deke's eyesight was so bad, even with his thick glasses, we were there almost an hour before he realized he had his own little audience. But after he discovered us, he'd grin at June Kipper and me between toots on his horn.

"Hey, man," June said, "he really blows!"

I was having a great time until I noticed that June kept casting these calf-eyed glances over toward Ruthie Scalese, standing with her sisters around the sawdust drum. It made me nervous as hell. But everything passed off okay, and finally the thing was over and me and June waited for Deke to collect his five dollars and then we all walked down to the DeLux Eat Shop in Sylvan Town, which was a little cluster of taxi stands and cafés near the college. Deke bought three Falstaff beers and we sat there and talked music for a while.

Deke said he had a half-pint of gin and thought he'd go down to the Canyon and see if he couldn't stir up a little jam session, and me and June could come along. But it was already past one A.M., so me and June begged off and went home. I would have given my left pinky to go down there and listen to the black guys and Deke jam, but it was a couple of years before I got to the Canyon for such activities. Maybe the wait was worth it. When I finally got into it, I didn't just listen, I blew a little, too. Not good, but plenty loud. Those guys in the Canyon really liked that. But that's another story.

June Kipper and me used to sit at one of the booths in the DeLux Eat Shop spooning up black-and-whites, which consisted of real vanilla ice cream in a soup bowl with a dose of chocolate syrup on top. At least, we spooned up the black-and-whites when there wasn't anybody around of age who'd buy us a Falstaff beer.

Anyway, we'd talk music. Hell, all we knew was the little bit we could play and what we'd heard on records.

I wish I could talk to him now, that June Kipper. Here we were, out of the hills of Arkansas, back in the days when anybody going as far away as Kansas City was a Big Deal. And since then?

Well, one day I would walk along Seventh Avenue in the city of New York, before Fifty-second Street became mostly Chinese eating joints and there was music there. And someday go into a place called Birdland and slip a twenty to this little black guy who was no taller than my hip pocket and thereby get seated at a table about the size of a modern-day credit card and on the stage would be Count Basie and his whole goddamned band, about ten thousand of them. At least it sounded like that many when they started blowing. Guys like Lockjaw Davis and Harry Edison and Joe Williams.

And so the bad part of all that was once I'd been there, once I'd tapped the real keg, it was past the time when I could sit in the DeLux Eat Shop spooning up black-and-whites and talking about the notes with June Kipper. Because, you see, he would have understood. He would have understood that these kinds of sounds are what the hell everything is all about.

But it never worked out that way.

What June Kipper and me had was each other, playing "In the Hall of the Mountain King" and "The Washington Post March" in the high school band. And we had the Cherokee Playboys and Aubrey Counts's band at the rec hall during summer months.

Some of those musicians we heard at the rec hall were top players, but by the time they ended up there, they were past the chance of ever playing again with the big names. Mostly because they couldn't stay sober and were deep into some weird substances.

Well, some were just old. Like a guy named Emmet something-or-other from Locust Grove, Oklahoma, who played enough clarinet to scare hell out of guys like Pee Wee Russell.

And Benny Strickler, who was dying of TB and who blew the sweetest trumpet I ever heard.

Benny lived right there in the county seat, and sometimes after school, June Kipper and me would go visit him and listen to him talk. He sat alone in this dark little room, the shades all drawn, and even in January he'd have an electric fan going. Benny's face was all pockmarked and that seemed to emphasize his wheezing breath and his whispered words. He wasn't much over thirty, I figured, but he looked old and eaten up inside and there was more to it than just the TB because he told us how he'd had his share of booze and pills and wild women in places like St. Louis and Chicago.

But he always talked clean and his hair was like a seventeen-year-old kid's, straight and light brown and stiff with vigor. Everything else was gone, inside and out. Except for his lips and his fingers on the valves.

Sometimes Benny would take out his horn, a thing that glowed with golden color in that shaded room, and slowly, with June Kipper and me watching and almost holding our breaths, he'd slip in the mouthpiece like it was some kind of sacred ritual and then lift the horn to his mouth and blow a few figures, gentle and soft and flowing like honey from the bell of that old trumpet.

And after he'd given us a little recital, he'd wheeze and slide the horn back into the long woolen sock he kept it in, and say, "Well, boys, I'm pretty tired now," and June Kipper and me would leave, feeling we'd had some sort of cleansing, like one of those old pilgrims whose feet had just been washed by the Holy Man.

So I guess June Kipper and me had more than "The Hall of the Mountain King" and the Cherokee Playboys. We had Benny Strickler, too.

Anyway.

I don't know how many times June Kipper and me went to the rec hall to listen. But somewhere along the line, I began to realize that June was going there for stuff besides the music. It was a suspicion I put out of my head because it scared hell out of me. But one day in the year before the war, when I was a senior in high school, I couldn't put it out of my head anymore because June pushed it right under my nose.

We were having a cherry malted milk at the Red Cross Drug Store, where they put crushed cherries in along with the syrup, waiting for the movie at the Palace Theater to start, and June turned to me with the straw stuck in the corner of his mouth.

"Hey, man, you get your mother's car now and then?"

"Well, sometimes," I said. "Depends on what I want it for."

"You think you could get it tomorrow night?"

"What the hell for?"

"It's important," he said. "It'll be worth your while."

So I made up some kind of excuse to my mother about needing the car so I could pick up a few friends and take them all to Wesley Hall at the Methodist church, where the Boy

Scouts of America, Troop 101, were having a lemonade-and-gingerbread reception as a sort of recruiting campaign. She bought the whole thing, even though she knew I was far past the age or inclination for Boy Scout recruitment.

I drove out to the Vets' Hospital about the time it was getting dark, and as soon as he got in the car, June Kipper handed me this Bach Nine mouthpiece for a baritone brass horn.

"It's got a long stem," he said, "so you gotta come way in with the tuning slide, but man, with this baby you can blow out the windows."

He said he got it from this guy up north who was a patient at the VA and who had played in the Detroit Symphony Orchestra.

"He's a patient?" I asked. "I ain't gonna catch anything from it, am I?"

"Hell, no, the guy's got cancer. You can't catch that from a mouthpiece."

The thing must have weighed a pound and I gave it a try and it fit my mouth like it was custom-made. I couldn't wait to get that thing in my old trombone.

Well, when somebody gives you something like that Bach Nine, you'd do anything for him without question. So when June Kipper told me to drive up to Tadmor, I drove, without a quiver of apprehension.

The apprehension came later, after dark, when he directed me to park at the side of the road, with grape vineyards on all sides and some mockingbirds making a lot of racket off in the distance. I turned off the lights and he got out and was gone without a word and right then I knew what the hell was going on.

Ruthie Scalese was what was going on. That little son of a bitch had come up here to meet her in one of the grape fields behind her daddy's house!

God only knows how many times I drove my mother's '36

Ford to Tadmor after dark so June Kipper and Ruthie Scalese could come together. It's really hell, what you'll do for a guy who gives you a Bach Nine mouthpiece. I didn't even want to think about it. So I just kept lying to get the car so I could take my friend out there in the night to do whatever it was he did with Ruthie among the Concords.

I don't know when or how June had the chance to talk with Ruthie and make these arrangements. I didn't want to find out. I was in so deep already, just being the taxi driver, and the last thing I needed was to have some big, mean Sicilian after my butt for contributing to the delinquency of his youngest daughter. And I was sure, without ever having the guts to ask, that June Kipper was probably doing more than just a little kissy-face in the grapevines.

I'd sit there in the dark in the '36 Ford, waiting for June to come back, and I'd think about it. A lot later in life, I read a sort of autobiography by some newspaper guy named Fowley or Fowler or something like that who claimed he'd never done the Thing with a woman until he was about twenty-four years old. It may be hard to believe now, in the era of promiscuous preteens, but not for anybody who remembers a hill town in 1940.

It was amazing. Here was June Kipper, the guy a lot of self-proclaimed studs who had never actually had their hands inside a girl's bloomers, much less anything else, said was a powderpuff, probably doing stuff in a grape vineyard that all the rest of us only dreamed about.

June had stopped going to those rec hall dances, but I'd been hooked, and almost every night there was music in the old sandstone building with the concrete dance floor, I was there. It was significant, I suppose, that Ruthie was always there too, giving me knowing looks, standing there beside the sawdust barrel with her sisters while her daddy and mama made fools of themselves on the floor and Old Tony sometimes getting excited and yelling, "Take it away, Leon," right along with the guys in the band.

I guess June Kipper had a sudden appetite for reading his text in solid geometry on dance nights, because he figured seeing Ruthie there amongst the jumpers and stompers would drive him crazy, knowing that in such a locale he couldn't run over there and grab her and kiss her and do any of those other things to which they had become accustomed. Whatever those things were.

This one night Deke Sanders was so hot I couldn't believe it. He was playing trombone like a maniac, and about eleven o'clock, an hour before the dance shut down, I was at the foot of the bandstand looking up and listening and Deke walked out to the front edge of the platform to do a solo. I think it was "San Antonio Rose."

Deke was a little drunk that night. In fact, Deke was stiffer than a boiled cat. His eyes behind the thick glasses were watery and glazed. But he came to the front of the bandstand and lifted his slush pump and started to play. He was blowing things I'd never heard before, and I was stomping my feet and yelling at him, egging him on.

Deke played and leaned forward, his eyes closed. The more he played, the more he leaned. And it suddenly came to me that owing to the law of gravity, which worked even in the rec hall, he'd never make it back to the upright position. And I was right.

It was a medley. They went from one thing to another, and when Deke really swayed out over the dance floor, they were doing "Honeysuckle Rose." Deke's favorite. Right in the middle of the best ride I ever heard him play, he just kept leaning. Like a pine tree cut at the base. He was as straight as a board, and he came right off the edge of that bandstand, horn blowing, eyes closed, and he kept right on coming, toward the concrete floor, lips tight against the mouthpiece.

My God, I'll never forget it. Deke played all the way down!

There was blood all over the place. Two of Deke's front teeth were knocked out and lying there on the dance floor along with the trombone, which now had a slide bent to look like a coat hanger. It was like there had been a knifing, and all the guys in the band stood up, even the piano guy, still playing away at "Honeysuckle Rose" and looking down to see what the hell had happened, and Deke staggered over to me and grabbed my shoulders in both his hands and he was bleeding like a stuck pig and laughing and saying it was the very best goddamned riff he'd ever blown.

Aubrey Counts came down off the bandstand and there were three deputy sheriffs clustered around him with their pistols sticking up out of their belts, and the dancers were standing back with their mouths open. Everybody was talking at once and the band was still playing and somewhere in all of this Deke let Aubrey Counts know that I blew a little trombone myself and that's when I got hired for my first professional job, standing right there with my shoe soles in Deke Sanders's blood and some jake-leg deputy sheriff holding me by the arm and yelling above the music, "What was it you done to this man, boy?"

Hell, you feel bad about a friend mutilating his lip so he can't play for a while. But it meant a job for me, so what's friendship got to do with it? So the next week, or whenever it was, there I sat with Aubrey Counts's Western swing band, blowing trombone. For a three-hour job I got five dollars for blasting out the only seventeen notes I knew on that Bach Nine mouthpiece. Why, it was a fortune!

But it was something better than money. I would have played for nothing, standing up there with all those guys, honking out a few things that would have shamed Deke Sanders or June Kipper, but the other musicians were stomping their feet while I played and yelling, "Take it away, Leon!"

That had come to mean more than a name. More than the Leon that played steel guitar with the Cherokee Playboys. It had come to mean encouragement for any guy who liked to blow, encouragement for a few good notes out of a lot of garbage, which is mostly what I played. Man, that was a long time ago and I can still hear those guys yelling.

Then it was spring. And for all of us who had turned eighteen or were about to, there was this restlessness brought on by the prospect of getting involved in something new and big and *important*. The new and big and *important* thing was World War II. I'd had my physical examination, at the invitation of the local draft board, and everything was all right so I knew that within a few weeks, as soon as our principal, Mr. Sylvester Longburn, handed me my diploma at the graduation exercises, I'd be headed straight as the railroad would take me into the army.

On this particular night, June Kipper and me were in the Smoke Shop having a chicken salad sandwich and a root beer float, and he was complaining about being left behind when everybody else went off to help whip the krauts and the Japs, just because he had bad feet and poor eyesight and some messed-up plumbing.

I thought for a while that I ought to tell him he was getting all the combat he needed in that Scalese vineyard, but decided against it. I never worked up the nerve to say anything to him about Ruthie, I don't know why.

It was just one of those ordinary evenings and outside there were people strolling around the square, window-shopping, and some early moving-picture-show folks were going up to the ticket window at the Palace Theater next door. We could hear one of the town mutts over on the post office lawn barking at cars that came by. So we finished our stuff and wheeled our butts off the counter stools and started for the door and that's when all hell broke loose. Because standing there glaring at us from beneath those big bushy black eyebrows was Antonio Scalese, and he looked pretty unhappy.

If the army could have seen June Kipper at that moment, they would have told him to come on in regardless of the bad feet and eyes and plumbing, because he showed more guts

than Eddie Rickenbacker. He walked right up to Tony Scalese
with his hand held out, blinking his blue eyes, and he spoke
in a clear voice that everybody in the Smoke Shop could hear.

"Mr. Scalese," June said, "my name's Kipper and my
daddy's a doctor and I'm 4-F in the draft but I hope you won't
hold that against me because I want to marry your daughter."

Old Tony just stood there a minute blinking, like somebody had punched him in the solar plexus, and then he let out
a roar and grabbed June Kipper like a sack of grape fertilizer
and threw him through the Smoke Shop screen door and out
onto the sidewalk, where all the people were queued up to
buy tickets at the Palace Theater. Then he charged out, still
roaring, while June got up and prepared to defend himself.

Well, when a guy has given you a Bach Nine mouthpiece
that was once in service with the Detroit Symphony, you
don't just stand by and watch him get massacred. Against my
better judgment, I jumped on Tony Scalese's back and put a
bear hug around his neck that I figured would choke the air
out of Tarzan of the Apes. Old Tony just reached back like
he was peeling off an undershirt and threw me against the grill
of a 1934 Chevrolet that was parked in front of the Palace
Theater. And as I picked myself off the chrome, I saw June
Kipper deliver the most ineffective blow I'd ever seen, square
against Old Tony's chin, and Old Tony roared again and
grabbed June and lifted him up and threw him against a glass
case on the wall that proclaimed to passersby that inside the
Palace Theater was playing a moving picture called *Waterloo
Bridge* with Vivien Leigh and Robert Taylor and that everybody should buy some popcorn on the way to their seats. The
glass shattered and the multicolored print of Vivien Leigh and
Robert Taylor getting ready to do some heavy kissing floated
out onto the sidewalk and lay there like a rumpled summer
dress among all the shards of glass.

Well, what the hell. June Kipper and me did the best we

could. People who had come to buy tickets or were just passing along the sidewalk expecting to evaluate the price of boots in the show window of Kennan's Shoe Emporium were scattering all over the place as the fight moved into the lobby of the Palace Theater. One of the ushers, this pimply-faced kid named Horace Elliot who must have figured because of the blue uniform he wore that he was a policeman, tried to stop it and got all the brass buttons on his coat torn off. Right after that the popcorn machine was totally destroyed and for a few minutes it looked like everything was happening in a snowstorm.

It's a long story, even though the action took a little less than five minutes. We taught some of the ladies who had been waiting to buy tickets to see Vivien Leigh and Robert Taylor a few words they'd never heard before. At least they likely told their husbands they'd never heard them. And finally, after wrecking the Palace Theater lobby, we ended up on the sidewalk again in front of Magowan's Drugstore, June Kipper and me sitting there and bleeding from various cuts and scrapes and Old Tony Scalese looking just like he had when it all started except that now, as he stood over us, there was a benevolent look on his Sicilian face.

There's only one thing about all that happened that I remember precisely. About the time the popcorn machine exploded, I heard June Kipper screaming and at the time I didn't even realize the screaming was about me and that it came when Old Tony had a fist cocked to give me what I suppose must have been his fifth or sixth lick against some part of my head.

What June Kipper was screaming was, "Don't hit him in the mouth, he's a horn player!"

Sometimes in the Ozarks we get these summer thunderstorms. They are furious and mindless and terrifying and then, in a tick, they're gone. That's how it was at the Palace Theater Massacre, as it came to be known.

Old Tony Scalese stood there a minute, looking down at June Kipper and me sitting on the sidewalk, and then he laughed a laugh I'll never forget.

"You kids got guts, I'll say that," he yelled. "But you little son of a bitch Kipper, I didn't come all the way down here from Tadmor to hear you tell me you were gonna marry my Ruthie. I come to tell *you*!"

Nobody ended up in jail. I guess Tony Scalese told the two town cops who arrived after it was too late for them to do anything that he'd pay for all the busted glass and the dismantled Smoke Shop screen door. Whatever, that big son of a bitch herded June Kipper and me into his old beat-up Dodge truck that had been double-parked through all the mayhem in front of the post office and took us home, me first, so I don't know what passed between them once I was let out and had to make up some kind of story to my mother about a split nose and a cheekbone going purple. I forget what the story was, because I told so many.

It's not that you enjoy lying to people you love. It's just that the more you love them, the more you want to protect them from all the foolish things you get yourself into.

For the next couple of weeks, until we graduated and guys like me were grabbed off by the army and sent on the Frisco to Camp Robinson to get ready to fight the War, there was the usual stuff between June Kipper and me. I didn't ask him anything and he didn't tell me anything about what he'd been doing with Ruthie Scalese or about what her old man had said to him. And so, before long, I was out of there and worrying about other large stuff, like how I could stay alive.

I'm ashamed to admit it, but for a long time I didn't give goat shit about what happened to June Kipper and Ruthie Scalese. I was too busy hiding under bulldozers and things like that when Jap airplanes came over dropping explosive stuff, wondering if my rifle would ever function again with all that goddamned sand in it.

After the War I came home, which was a plus because a lot of guys who went off on that train with me at the start didn't. Anyway, I found out the old rec hall had been spliced up into offices, partitions built right on the concrete dance floor. My good friend Emmy Joe Gorman's stepdaddy had an office there, and the day I went in to pay my respects, only Emmy Joe was there, his stepdaddy being in court at the time, and we shot the shit. Emmy Joe sat behind his stepdaddy's desk with his feet up like he was already a real-life lawyer, and I sat in one of those big chairs along the far wall, the kind that was supposed to make clients feel like everything was no sweat even if there'd been seventeen witnesses to their having beat their wife to death with a baseball bat.

We grinned at each other a lot, me and Emmy Joe. Then he started telling me how he'd whipped the krauts single-handed. And then I told him how I'd done the same thing to the Japs. It was a helluva conversation.

And then somehow, like it always was between old friends seeing each other after a long tiresome time, there wasn't anything more to say. So to make conversation, I asked about June Kipper.

"Oh," says Emmy Joe. "He's still down in South America, working with one of those oil companies."

"The hell you say."

"Yeah," says Emmy Joe. "He went to the university and got to be one helluva linguist."

"The hell you say."

"Yeah. Him and Ruthie got four kids now. I hear all about him. My stepdaddy tells me about it. Ruthie's old man, he's a client of my stepdaddy."

"The hell you say."

"Yeah, Old Tony got his ass in a sling a couple years ago. My stepdaddy defended him."

"Defended him for what?"

"Murder in the first," says Emmy Joe, and I couldn't help thinking about that night in front of the Palace Theater when me and June Kipper decided to take a few shots at this big Sicilian.

"Yeah?"

"Not guilty," says Emmy Joe. "After they closed this place, they opened a Legion Hut up in Tadmor. A lot smaller. Old Tony butchered some guy right on the dance floor. A very big knife. Some Tulsa band was playing."

"What the hell was Old Tony's beef?"

"A guy was trying to make one of his daughters," Emmy Joe says. "Hey. There were two hundred seventy-four witnesses. But when the action took place, they were all in the john and didn't see a thing."

"A big john, huh?"

We both laughed.

And I thought some more about the time outside the Palace Theater when me and June Kipper were discussing things with Tony Scalese. Man, I could remember. Right here where I was sitting talking to my good friend Emmy Joe Gorman, and June Kipper cutting those calf eyes toward Ruthie Scalese and Deke Sanders blowing his brains out on the trombone and the smell of sawdust and thirty-eight deputy sheriffs standing around with nickel-plated pistols just waiting to bop you on the head, and Bobby Lew Hillspeth trying to keep his musicians from beating hell out of each other between sets.

God, what a time it had been.

So me and Emmy Joe both laughed, without saying much, there in his stepdaddy's law office where there had once been considerable action and me scraping the soles of my shoes on that same concrete floor.

"Got acquitted, did he?" I said, meaning Old Tony Scalese.

"Yeah."

And we both laughed and I could begin to smell the sawdust from the barrels and hear the hum of those bugs around the gooseneck lamp at the front door and feel the humping throb of that music when the hardcases were jumping up and down with their women.

"Take it away, Leon," I said, and we both laughed some more.

9

Trusty

Sometimes, enterprising jour-
nalists or historical researchers will track down and inter-
view the kind of extraordinary characters that seem so
unusual they should only exist in novels. Some people stum-
ble across such misfits by chance. Shanks Caulder seemed to
do an awful lot of that. The people with whom he has been
associated over six decades of life are so unusual you'd think
they'd been mined, like rare and semiprecious stones. And
although he might never admit such a thing, each and every
one of them has had an effect on his life. As Shanks has said,
every one of us is a little part of everybody else we know, like
it or not, saints and sons of bitches.

Shanks Caulder is about half policeman, half criminal.
Perhaps the difference between the two is not so great as
would appear at first glance. And perhaps that accounts for
Shanks's understanding that there's not much dividing line
in any of us between what might be called Bible-good and
what is most certainly Satan-wicked.

"It's like a dice game," Shanks has often said, perched on
his egg crate and fishing sardines out of a can with a tooth-
pick. "You roll and sometimes it comes up nice and some-

185

times it comes up sticky. The thing is, with most people when it comes up sticky they never get caught at it.''

Shanks would say that everyone he has ever known was "only normal.'' Running down the list of his acquaintances, some serious arguments might be made to the contrary.

Have you ever heard of a guy named something like Lilus Pront? If you did, you'd figure this guy for a big pussycat, a poor devil who likely got his butt whipped each day in school by some stud named Butch Dong.

Well, Lilus Pront was one of the gentlest men I ever met. And one of the most deadly. And nobody, whether his name was Butch Dong or whatever, ever whipped his ass.

Lilus Pront was the best example I ever knew of a guy who made the system work, no matter the odds. Because he knew when to lie to it, still smiling his gentle smile and shaking his

head and saying it's the best goddamned system known to
man. Even if now and again you have to lie to make it work.

I met Lilus Pront when I was a junior in high school, before juniors in high school were sniffing coke and knew more
about sexual gymnastics than their parents. In other words, a
long time ago.

It was a time of chaperoned dances and sending gardenia
corsages to your date and dancing to recorded stuff by Glen
Miller and Harry James and maybe even a few of those dorks
like Guy Lombardo and Sammy Kaye. And smelling the new
asphalt they were laying on city streets that had always been
gravel. And guys going to parties at girls' houses where post
office was played and maybe you'd get a chance to kiss
somebody—a girl, that is—square on the lips. And it was a
time when you were sweating out the grade you'd get on last
week's theme in English Three and going to the pool hall after
school to watch all these old guys play a game called Moon,
with dominoes, talcum powder all over their hands and all
over the table, the whole place smelling of stale Falstaff beer,
and behind all the rest of the noise, those ivory balls clicking
against one another on the snooker tables.

And some guy would yell, "Rack!" and throw his quarter
on the green felt table to pay for the game and the other guy
at the table would grin and shove the ten bucks he'd just won
on the game into his hip pocket and then chalk up his cue with
one of those little blue cubes.

Hell, in those young days that pool hall was another world
and you wondered if you'd ever join in. And then, years later,
after you had, you'd wish you could get out of it somehow.

And there was more innocent stuff, like watching Miss
Fraser's bottom move in that mysterious way when she
walked up to the blackboard and started writing something,
all the boys in the room not giving a damn what it was she
wrote, just so long as she stood there swinging that thing. And
going over across the street from the high school at noon and

hearing all the bad, bad stories the football players told, and buying penny cigarettes at Rufus Blair's store and watching the sun go down toward Oklahoma in a red haze and wondering if you'd ever grow up. Six feet tall, and still a kid. A hundred sixty pounds, and still a kid, you'd think.

There were bluebirds then, too. Real bluebirds that were the blue of ocean water around one of those islands you'd seen on postcards, with a bright orange breast. There aren't very many bluebirds around anymore.

It was one night in the spring of that year when Hitler was raising hell in Germany and we'd go to the moving-picture show and watch these guys goose-stepping with a lot of torches and smoke and we'd think, Jesus, someday we'll have to fight those guys, and it was the spring when the local national guard outfits were oiling up their howitzers and getting ready to be called to active federal service, and it was the spring when the Castle Lunch was selling a bag of five hamburgers for a dollar and when somebody walked out of there carrying the grease-stained sack you could smell it all the way to the courthouse a block away. Hamburgers don't smell like that anymore. They mostly smell like hot felt nowadays.

Anyway.

It was a time when the juices were really flowing through the blood veins, the kinds of juices that make the boys pant a little and the girls blush and the cold of winter evaporate in one gentle breeze through the budding dogwood.

So on this night, Duny Jordan and me decided we'd go out to the Lilac Club and listen to Emmy Joe Gorman's stepdaddy and all the other guys blow some music, and have some fun getting a little boiled and watching the grown-up ladies doing the same thing and dancing around the floor like hell wasn't only tomorrow away.

Duny Jordan and me, we played in the high school band, him trumpet, me trombone. He was a sweet kid. He introduced me to cigarette smoking with a cup of coffee in the mornings at his house after I'd spent the night with him. Even when he was a kid, a cigarette and a cup of coffee was all the breakfast Duny Jordan ever had. I was more inclined toward pork sausage and gravy and three or four sunny-side-up eggs.

On these expeditions, there were the economics to consider. That is, after we'd made some excuse to get out of the house without our mothers really knowing where we were headed, we needed at least a dollar each, for a total of two, saved up from mowing lawns or pitching newspapers. A dollar went for a half-pint of gin. Then a quarter each for the Lilac Club cover charge. Then the remaining two quarters for a bottle of beer each, chaser for the gin. It brought on a pretty good buzz. Enough at least so that we could walk back into town along the highway, singing dirty songs and giggling and talking about the ladies we'd watched on the dance floor and making up somewhat carnal fantasies about them.

We figured this was all right, Duny Jordan and me, even if we were still just high school kids. We were special, you see, like we weren't controlled by other people's rules. This was because we were musicians and knew who Sid Catlett was, for Christ's sake, and nobody but people like us knew such things. So we figured it was okay if now and again on a spring Saturday night we would get a little gouged on gin and beer. In fact, Duny Jordan had memorized that poem by Kipling that goes, "You can talk of gin and beer, when you're quartered safe out here." Or something like that.

On this particular night, I walked into Sheldon Backer's liquor store and threw down my dollar and said I wanted a half-pint of gin. And Sheldon Backer, a guy we called Tiger because that had been his name when he'd been a professional boxer, just looked at me and shook his head.

"Kid," he said, "I can't sell you no juice."

I said something to the effect that such a disaster had not occurred since the Jamestown Flood and he said the law was looking down his neck for selling juice to minors and seemed particularly disturbed about his loading the trunk of his Lincoln with booze each weekend and driving over into Oklahoma and selling it at outlandish prices, Oklahoma at that time being as dry as a Baptist parsonage.

"Well, shit," I said, or something like that, and Tiger was looking mournful and he saw Duny Jordan peeking into his front window from the sidewalk, looking like a little Christmas elf, and Tiger drew a deep breath.

"I'll tell you what I'll do, kid," he said. "If you and Duny wanta hang around for about an hour, I'll be closing and I'll take you out to the Rocky Palace and buy you a beer."

You might think Tiger Backer was crazy, offering to buy some beer for Duny Jordan and me if the law was really looking down his neck. But he wasn't that stupid. The Rocky Palace was the toughest place in four counties, and city cops never stuck their noses in there unless there was a serious shooting or knifing, which there was from time to time, and then only in full force and with half a dozen deputy sheriffs with shotguns to back them up. It was that kind of place.

I told Tiger that Duny Jordan and me appreciated his offer but that the Rocky Palace wasn't exactly our idea of the kind of place to spend a quiet evening getting tagged from the juice.

"Hell, kid, you'll be with me," he said, grinning the little grin he had that made his flattened box fighter's nose turn in the direction of his right ear. "Besides, you're always hangin' out around the courthouse and seem interested in evildoers, so I thought you might like to meet a guy I'm gonna see out there."

"What kind of guy?" I asked.

"A guy who has spent a lot of hard time at Cummins," Tiger said.

That sold me. Because Cummins was known among courthouse hangers-on as the meanest, toughest, killingest penitentiary in the whole wide world, and just seeing a guy who'd spent hard time there and was still alive to think about it was better than going to the circus. I knew it was a special favor that Tiger was offering because he liked me.

The reason Tiger liked me was because at that time I was a boxing crazy. Joe Louis was my hero. I always went to the moving-picture show when they were playing the Brown Bomber's latest fight. I saw so many of those things I began to imagine I'd figured out how to do it myself until one night in the National Guard Armory they had a Boy's Club fight card and matched me in the four-round main event with a kid named Buck Burtom.

The fight lasted thirty seconds into the second round, by which time I figured I was in front on points from these sneaky little body blows I was getting into Buck's ribs. Trouble was, sometimes I'd throw a right and forget to keep the left up in front of my chin. I saw the punch coming, but there wasn't anything I could do about it. I woke up three hours later sitting in the Palace Theater with a bunch of my friends watching something called *Tarzan Returns*.

Later on I got to know Buck Burtom pretty well, and he was a nice guy. I helped one of his sisters elope because on the night she and her boyfriend decided on the big step, I happened to have the family car for a Methodist Youth Meeting, or some such thing. I forget exactly what it was, but I'll never forget exactly how hard Buck Burtom could hit. And if he'd caught me that night I drove his sister and her new husband to a tourist cabin in Benton County, he'd probably have reminded me.

Buck was killed in a car accident, or else during the War. There were so many guys in my high school that went one way or the other that it's hard to remember, so I don't try anymore.

Anyway, Tiger Backer had been in New York the night Joe Louis fought Max Baer, who Tiger said was maybe the best heavyweight around if he'd only learned to keep away from booze and women and bright lights when he should have been skipping rope.

"Baer was wide awake in the fourth when he went down and stayed," Tiger would tell me for the thousandth time. "But he had sense enough not to get up. He may have been a big-assed playboy, but he wasn't all the way stupid."

Then Tiger was there again when Louis creamed Max Schmeling in their second fight. I would go to Tiger's liquor store after I'd seen the slow-motion movies of that fight and he'd relate it all, blow by blow, and me all the while doing a poor imitation of the Louis left hook among the stacks of Old Grand Dad and Gordon's gin.

"That Joe," I'd say, "always clean living and no women or juice and reads his Bible every night."

Hell, I'd read it in all the newspapers. But Tiger, when I said such things, would look at me with a funny expression on his face and shake his head like he knew better. But he never stuck a pin into my bubble and it took me a lot of years to find out that my box-fight hero enjoyed some of the same excitements of the flesh that all the rest of us do.

I should have listened more closely to Tiger on a lot of things. He'd said, "Hey, kid. You got good sloping shoulders, so you could hit pretty hard if you developed it, and you got a pretty strong neck. But a real puncher is gonna find that glass jaw you got."

Which Buck Burtom proved correct in a little under four minutes of combat.

So much for my career in the fight game. At least I got to see the last half of *Tarzan Returns* for free because one of my friends felt so sorry for me after I got knocked out that he bought my ticket to the show. And I learned that a guy can move around and act like he's still in this world and not recall a minute of it later on. Jesus. That Buck Burtom could hit!

Anyway.

On the night in question, Duny Jordan and me ended up at the Rocky Palace with Tiger Backer, Duny Jordan and me trying to act casual among all those big guys with tattoo art on their arms and scars on their knuckles. And we met Lilus Pront.

It was a little bit disappointing, to say the least. Lilus Pront was just an average-sized man with baby-blue eyes and a nice mouth and a square jaw and he was wearing a suit that looked like it probably cost fifteen dollars, and a wrinkled white shirt, and a necktie, and a pair of shoes so scuffed and run over at the heels that you figured just looking at them that they'd seen a lot of sidewalk mileage.

We sat in this booth in one corner of the Rocky Palace, and as soon as we were settled and Tiger had beers all around, Lilus Pront pulled out a briefcase with samples of sterling tableware and tried to sell me a set.

"You love your mother, don't you?" he said, smiling a gentle little smile. "You could pay if off on time."

I couldn't figure out why Tiger Backer would be so interested in such a pillow-soft guy as Lilus Pront. But then, after Duny Jordan and me had swilled down three beers, Duny made some kind of remark one of the resident hard-necks at the Rocky Palace didn't like and he came over with his tattoos gleaming and started to explain all the various ways he was about to tear Duny's high school balls right off his belly and stuff them into Duny's mouth.

Halfway through this recitation of mayhem, Lilus Pront stood up. He didn't say a word. He just looked at this guy with the tattoos, who must have outweighed him by at least eighty pounds. But Lilus Pront looked him dead square in the face and this guy took a couple of swallows and turned around and walked away and Lilus Pront sat down and went back to trying to sell me a four-place setting of sterling silver.

When a thing like that happens, you have to take a closer look. But with Lilus Pront, all I could see was a sort of seedy citizen just like one you might see walking out of church on Sunday or the bank on Monday. Except that when he stood up to face that guy who was going to rip off Duny Jordan's manhood with his bare hands, there had been a change. As though the face of Lilus Pront had turned to cold solid rock and his eyes to hot metal.

On the Fourth of July, little kids were always burning sparklers. And when the dazzling silver fire was gone, the things would glow red, and if you stepped on one with a bare foot it meant a helluva lot of screaming and heavy slathers of zinc-oxide ointment. Well, when Lilus Pront stood up that night in the Rocky Palace, his eyes had looked like that burnt sparkler. Dead, but still hot enough to sear the flesh off a bare foot.

Tiger Backer drove Duny Jordan and me back into town about one A.M. and I said Lilus Pront hadn't seemed like much of an ex-con to me.

"He don't talk much about it," said Tiger Backer.

The hell he didn't. I found out later that Lilus Pront would talk your leg off about Cummins if you showed any interest. Of course, I didn't find out this fact until almost thirty years later, by which time I had forgotten all about Lilus Pront.

It was after the Charlie War. The one in Southeast Asia where the guys in the black pajamas didn't ever come out until what they called the Tet Offensive and we butchered their asses and everybody in the States said it was a terrible setback for our side. Jesus.

Anyway, it was time to get out and do a little fishing, so that's what I did, and by then they had all these dams along White River and they'd stocked the water just below the dams with rainbow trout so a guy could catch striped bass from the lake and two hours later pull in trout downstream, using canned corn on a hook for bait. Something about those big yellow kernels of corn drove those transplanted trout crazy.

So one mid-afternoon I'm standing on the dock of a marina and this nice-looking little guy walks up smiling and holds out his hand and says, "Well. I guess you don't know me."

And I didn't but figured this wasn't a touch of some sort

because this guy was wearing a jumpsuit of excellent fiber and a pair of high-polished shoes that must have cost about eighty dollars and there was a big diamond ring on his right pinky.

"I'm Lilus Pront," he said.

It's a little spooky sometimes when suddenly somebody yanks open a door to your high school years, a door that hasn't been opened in one helluva long time. So I'm standing there smelling the old fish smell of that marina and feeling the sun on my neck and the glare of it on the water of the lake and shaking the hand of this little dude that had once tried to sell me a four-place setting of sterling silver.

God, he looked so small. It was like the time I came home from the War and walked into my grandmother's living room, which had always been the biggest, grandest room in all creation but was then suddenly a dinky, dingy, poorly lit matchbox.

What the hell. I asked him over to my car where I had a fifth of Jack Daniel's and we sat there and sipped a few and puffed cigarettes for chasers, and he asked me about all the stuff that had happened to me since that night in the Rocky Palace and I told him it would be like reciting the entire text of the *Encyclopaedia Britannica* just to get well started on the first war, not to mention the two after that, and he laughed and invited me over to his place, which wasn't too far, in one of those communities that had sprouted up around the lakes, sort of motel rooms with a deck and a dog and within a short drive to the closest mall, where you could buy your booze and shrimp and plastic shoes.

It was a nice little place. Brick veneer. Two bedrooms and one full bath and a patio paved with red tile and a tiny green lawn all around. And a carport with a boat sitting there on a trailer, and right in front of that a Chevy pickup truck with a rifle rack across the back window.

Lilus Pront had this little wife, too, whose name was Loutie, and she hustled us into the den where there were a few

Mickey Spillane paperbacks scattered around and a TV and a magazine rack with some unopened *National Geographics* and a plastic beer cooler with a red top. Lilus Pront sat there in a recliner chair and I sat in a big armchair that swallowed me, and we waited for Loutie to bring some glasses to pour our Jack Daniel's into and he smiled at me.

So I mentioned Cummins. Just in passing, because it didn't make any difference to me anymore—I'd seen enough hard-cases in thirty years that I figured one more was no big deal. But I was wrong, and Lilus Pront told me all about his life, as though I was his preacher and he could bare his soul without any inhibitions or shame. It's one helluva scary feeling when a guy does that to you.

"It's all women," he said, smiling. Jesus, the guy was always smiling. "A woman got me into trouble. Another one kept me there. And finally, the one you just met got me out of it. It's a helluva story. I may write a book about it."

Before it was over I went out and bought some more Jack Daniel's and two cases of beer. I think it was Coors because at the time Coors seemed to be the thing to do, although I've never really understood why.

The year after the Great War, Lilus Pront was coming into his manhood. He was doing this by working part-time as a garage mechanic and full-time as a bootlegger in south Arkansas. Somewhere along the line he saved enough money to buy a used Indian motorcycle with a chain drive. Almost every night he would roar around visiting the roadhouses where everybody was sopping up as much booze as they could before the Volstead Act became the law of the land by constitutional amendment in January 1920. After that, it turned out, people continued to sop up the booze in the same roadhouses in a sort of frantic race to outdo one another in violating Prohibition.

But by then, Lilus Pront was out of circulation.

He became heavily involved with a young lady in one of

these roadhouses. She was about fifteen years older than him—he was then on the push side of nineteen. On one of his nocturnal jaunts, he discovered that there was another stud contending for this lady's affections. A scuffle ensued. There were shots fired.

"The son of a bitch pulled a knife on me," Lilus Pront told the judge.

However, when the deputy sheriffs arrived at the scene, they found no knife on or about the body sprawled before the bar. What they found was three closely spaced .45-caliber holes in this guy's shirtfront. Lilus Pront was hauled off to jail with appropriate jolts to the head and neck, which policemen of that time delivered in the line of official duty with such things as fists, pistol barrels, and tire irons.

Arraigned for second-degree murder, Lilus Pront received the mercy of the court. He was on probation for an assault rap two years before, and upon learning this, the judge, in his zeal to protect the county's taxpayers from unnecessary court costs, just imposed the max for the first offense and fed Lilus Pront to the Arkansas penal system for a period of twenty-one years.

"And God have mercy on you," the judge said, "because when you get down there to Cummins, they sure as hell won't."

The sheriff of Grant County drove Lilus to the pen in his own Model T Ford.

"When we pulled up in front of the administration building at Cummins," Lilus said, "sheriff handed me a deck of smokes. He says, 'Ain't fer smoking. Fer payin' dues.' I didn't know what the hell he meant, but I found out."

And I found out, too, only not firsthand like Lilus Pront had done. It was a little scary, thinking about such things happening to people in my own native state when I was just a kid worrying about not much except a little constipation now and then or the blue jays in our backyard that attacked me with dive-bombing sweeps when they had young in their nests, or the mean little bastard kid down the street who smashed a raw egg on my head one day.

The Cummins prison farm was run like a feudal dungeon except that it was mostly out in the open, flat fields with dusty or muddy roads, depending on the season, radiating out from the barracks to the cultivated tracts where the convicts worked in the various crops, cotton and black-eyed peas and spinach. The whole thing was run by the convict trusties. They were the only armed guys around. The three or four state employees, the "free world" guys, never carried any weapon at all. These guys were called "whipping bosses" because they were the ones who used the long leather straps to beat hell out of the cons. But the people who indicated which cons were to be whipped were just other cons. The trusties, you see?

"Hell," Lilus Pront said. "There was a trusty boss for everything and the cons had to keep them happy with a few cigarettes or money or whatever other favors they might have to offer. Else you'd get your ass whipped. It's a funny thing, after a few licks of that leather strap, you could feel the pain running up to the base of your skull like a hot needle. Not a big, broad pain, just a sharp little needle that could drive you crazy when you were lying there on the ground and the whipping boss was coming down on you for the next lick and you knew it was going to hurt, man. And sometimes they'd wait a few seconds, knowing you were braced for it, and then whip it down on you again and you knew they expected you to beg. They always expected that. To see you beg and cringe like a dog and spit out all the dignity you had just to keep him from hitting you anymore."

"Like what other kinds of favors?" I asked.

"Like maybe sex. But not much. I don't think there was as much of that then as there is now," Lilus Pront said, smiling his little smile and taking another sip of Jack Daniel's.

"Those guys who worked the Long Line every day were too damned tired to think about sex. Too scared, too, because sex was just for the trusties. And hell, the trusties could leave the farm any night they wanted and go to one of the little shacks close by and get a real woman."

Then he laughed again, this time a real belly-shaking laugh.

"We even had a whorehouse. Right there. A few of the guys who would do any damned thing for a few cigarettes or bucks, they made a little nest above the mess hall. And on Sunday, when it was visiting day, they'd be up there in the attic accepting visitors all afternoon. The trusties got their slice of the action. Whatever our little man-whores made on a Sunday afternoon, they had to share it with the trusties, and some of the free-world guys, too."

If a man got in bad with a mess-hall trusty boss, he didn't eat too well. If he got in bad with a barracks trusty boss, he didn't sleep too well, if at all. And he couldn't buy a Coke or a candy bar from the commissary that was at the end of each barracks, separated from the rows of army cots by heavy chain-link wire and consisting of a soft-drink cooler that sometimes had ice, and a rack of Tootsie Rolls and Brown Mule chewing tobacco along one wall and a stand on the floor for three or four .30-30 Winchesters.

But the very worst guy to get in bad with was the Long Line rider.

When the cons went out to work the fields, for which the state paid them seven cents an hour, they called it the Long Line because the cons were positioned at the edge of the cotton patch or whatever, in a long line. When the Long Line rider gave the command, they began to move through the rows of growing stuff and if a guy couldn't keep up with the rest of the men, he was in for a whipping.

"You picked cotton like a maniac," Lilus Pront said. "Just to keep up. Because the rider was always watching. New guys would have fingers bleeding before noon, you know, before their hands got toughened to it, and they'd fall behind. And they'd get the shit beat out of them because they couldn't keep up. It was a real holiday."

The rider had some business enterprises, too. Once each morning and once each afternoon, the coffee cart came out, with a little cold toast and maybe sometimes even a dough- nut bag. If you had a few pennies or a cigarette for the rider, you'd get coffee. If a man was fresh out of such things, he just lay down in the cotton rows and tried to dry off the sweat and he didn't get a damned thing.

"Hell," Lilus Pront said, "we had a water wagon there all the time on the Long Line. But if you were a guy who was really in wrong with the rider, you didn't even get that, all day long, in the hot sun. You didn't even get water unless you could pay a little for it. You know, there's all kinds of ways to commit murder."

So it came to me slowly that a con could be killed without much effort. And besides that, there was the whipping boss.

This guy, who was a free-world employee of the state, would arrive at the field once each morning, once each after- noon. He'd generally come out in a Model T Ford driven by a convict trusty. He'd spit and smoke and cuss a little with the rider. Then, after a while, the rider would call out a man on the Long Line that he didn't like or that he thought hadn't been keeping up too well, and the con would spread-eagle himself in the dirt road and the employee of the sovereign state would beat the hell out of him with one of those leather straps.

Sometimes a man couldn't survive this kind of treatment. So he was just buried in a shallow grave alongside the cotton rows. Or dumped into the Arkansas River.

"When we heard the trusties talking about a guy being tur- tle bait," Lilus Pront said, "we knew he might last a month. Maybe a little longer. But man, he was dog meat when the trusties wanted him to be, sooner or later."

On the Long Line, they had trusties with shotguns. They stood in pretty close to the cons working the crops. Back some distance from them were the trusties on horseback. They had rifles. The idea was that if one of the con trusties with a shotgun tried to break, the guys on horseback with rifles could outrange him and blow his ass away. It was a hierarchy of trusty power. And the biggest power of all was the Long Line rider, who had the best horse and the best rifle and knew how to use it.

"Why, a man would cut his own mother's throat just to survive," Lilus Pront said. "That was it, you see. Surviving one more day. One more day. And the Long Line rider was God Almighty. When you put men in that situation, all the free-world bullshit doesn't mean anything anymore. It's just get through one more day. It's just live, man, no matter how you can, no matter who you squash along the way."

It was almost a sure-fire cinch to get a parole by killing another con trying to escape. So getting trusty status, with a gun, was very big. It meant that the Long Line rider and every trusty below him made a science of harassing the other men in hopes one would get so insane with it he'd try to make a break.

"We didn't need any of them sweat boxes you see in the movies all the time. You sweat a man in a box, he just stays in there and dies. You gouge him all the time out in the open and that near tree line starts looking closer and closer. And out there, if he runs, you can dust him."

It turned out this little angel-faced man I knew, with the nice blue eyes and the ready smile, had been one tough cookie. But he was something else besides. He was smart. He worked himself upward in the system, paying out his cigarettes and calling the free-world guys "boss" and spending the few dollars his old daddy sent him in the right places. He stayed out of trouble with the Long Line rider and the barracks bosses. He'd had a little education and he remembered some of it.

"Why, hell, most guys in the pen when I was there couldn't even write their names," he said. "And I'm talking about white guys. The jigs were in a separate place. I mean, hell, our barracks and fields were white as the driven snow, like they say."

After about a year, Lilus Pront ended up in the administration building, as a trusty, and thereby became the most powerful man in the system.

What the hell, you say. He didn't have a rifle. He didn't ride a horse behind the Long Line. He didn't point out other cons for punishment by the whipping bosses. It's all true, but what he had was control of the records of every convict in the whole state penal system.

For a fee from any one of the other inmates, he could make little alterations, so that a guy who had raped his baby sister and strangled his mother for objecting ended up on paper looking like an ordained Baptist minister. And you see, those were the records that went before the parole board when a guy came up for his hearing.

Listen, Lilus Pront became penitentiary rich and had power to burn.

There was more. Because he handled the files, he was expected to appear at each meeting of the parole board in Little Rock, carrying those documents with him and making recommendations about the advisability of releasing a mad-dog killer back on society or keeping him on the Long Line.

"As far as the cons were concerned," Lilus Pront said, "I had more power than the governor. You'd be surprised how little erasing it took to change a con's record, and those board members never looked at any of the paper. They just asked me. So if the changes were a little messy sometimes, nobody knew the difference. And the few free-world guys at the prison, hell, they never looked, either. I think maybe some of those bastards couldn't read."

The State of Arkansas bought him an eighteen-dollar suit so he'd look respectable when he was at those board meetings. And another trusty drove him into Little Rock, about sixty miles from Cummins, on the days the board sat. And after the few hours the board met, Lilus Pront and the other con would go on the town, such as it was, getting drunk and having a whore before they went back to the pen in a day or two.

It was a helluva deal.

So finally, with the help of his eraser and a lot of imagination, Lilus Pront worked his own record into pretty good shape and got paroled himself. But there was more to it than that.

"I got this big chance when there was a prison break and I asked to go along with the posse. I'd been in about eight years then," Lilus Pront said. "There weren't many breaks from Cummins because the guys knew that when they got caught—and they almost always did—they'd get a .30-30 slug up the nose, no questions asked.

"This posse cornered two of the escapees in an old sharecrop shack. The deputy sheriffs and the state cops blasted away at this shack for a long time. At first the two cons inside shot back, because they were well armed. Then, after a while, no more shots came from the shack.

"Everybody hemmed and hawed a while about what to do, so I said, 'Gimme a shotgun and I'll go in there and look.' So I did. The inside of that place looked like a Swiss cheese. In a slaughterhouse. Blood all over the place, and both cons dead as nails on the floor.

"What the hell. I didn't have to think very long about it. I just let off two blasts of that shotgun into the floor and then hollered out that they could come in and scrape up the bodies.

"They figured I'd gone in there and killed these two cons myself, so the next time the parole board met, I was a cinch for the free world. Thanks to a state-owned shotgun and my own little eraser."

The day he got out, in one of those ex-convict suits the system provided, Lilus Pront headed straight for Little Rock and a woman named Ruby he'd met during one of those parole board meeting binges. She considered that Arkansas wasn't big enough for Lilus Pront's talents, so they took a bus for East St. Louis, Illinois.

"Sure, I was supposed to report to a parole office," Lilus Pront told me. "But hell, in those days such stuff was pretty loose. And Ruby said if I didn't take her to a big town she was going back to Texas and find an oilman. And Ruby was a comfortable lay. And still being young and stupid, I was willing to put my whole life on the line for the sake of a comfortable lay."

In East St. Louis, Lilus Pront became a bag man for the mob. He had good credentials. So they hired him to go to all the whorehouses once a week and collect the sackful of protection money, which he then delivered to a representative of the local police department, in order, as Lilus Pront put it, that the free-enterprise system among the love-starved could continue without interruption from the men in blue, or whatever the heat wore in East St. Louis, Illinois, in 1930.

"Then they had an election," Lilus Pront said. "And there was a new bunch of politicians who had won on a reform ticket, but the minute the votes were counted they had their hands out for the green in the brown bags. And of course they wanted their own guys in the collection end of things."

Every time there was a crime of any sort, like rape or robbery or murder or indecent exposure in East St. Louis, Illinois, Lilus Pront found himself scooped up by the cops and slapped into a lineup. It didn't take him long to figure out that sooner or later some bleary-eyed citizen would put the finger on him for something he hadn't done.

"At least the mob guys didn't hire some goon to penetrate my gut with an icepick," he said. "They worked it so I'd get the idea that my welcome had worn out in East St. Louis, Illinois, and I'd just evaporate. Which I did. Ruby, the comfortable lay, had taken up with some greasy punk who bragged about being a friend of Al Capone, up in Chicago. And besides, that East St. Louis, Illinois! I never liked the fucking place.''

So he came back to Arkansas and tried to sell place settings of sterling silver. He didn't sell a single teaspoon. So he thought about heisting a filling station or two, but didn't. Then he got involved with two guys who rustled cattle, and the very first night on that job he almost emasculated himself on a barbed-wire fence trying to get the damned critters out of their pen and onto an old bob truck.

So he decided to try insurance. He just walked into a place after stealing a good suit right off the rack at a Sears, Roebuck, and asked for a job and told them he'd been wounded in the war and had no criminal record and his mother, who had actually been dead for fifteen years, was suffering from TB, and that he owned a lot of property in Mississippi and that he was a member of the Baptist church.

"Son of a bitch," he said, laughing. "They hired me. And I sold so much damned insurance in six months they gave me a raise and within two years I was the head guy at one of their agencies.''

"Did you tell them? About Cummins?" I asked.

"I was vice-president of a regional office when I finally told my boss. Hell, that was many a year after I'd stopped carrying a pistol even to the moving-picture show or had tried to murder anybody," Lilus Pront said. "So he asked me why I hadn't come clean with the company from the start and I asked if I had, would they have hired me, and he said no, and we had a drink of Canadian VO and that was the end of it. Now I'm retired and a respected member of the community.''

Well, I said I could see how a couple of women had been bad news in early years, but where did the last one come in, and he said he'd met Loutie the first year he was selling insurance. Even then, every time he passed a Texaco station he'd wonder about how much money was in the drawer, that being a long time before they started using these plastic cards, and he'd halfway plan coming back at closing time with a .45.

But once he'd met Loutie, it was all over.

"I loved that woman so much," Lilus Pront said. "Sometimes at night when she was sleeping, I'd just lay there looking at her face and think how nice it would have been if I'd known her in those days when I was riding an old Indian motorcycle and peddling bootleg whiskey. Of course, she wasn't even born then."

It was about that time when Loutie herself walked into the den and said Lilus Pront and me had been talking a long time and maybe needed some chow and that she had some pork sandwiches and potato salad and that maybe we'd had enough of that high-calorie stuff like whiskey and beer and maybe now we ought to have a glass of cold milk.

After we ate, Lilus Pront walked me out to my car. It was a long time dark and there was a moon. We shook hands and I could see Lilus Pront smiling at me.

"Come back sometime," he said, and likely knew I never would. And then he said something about Tiger Backer and that he'd gone to Tiger's funeral. I was on Okinawa then.

"I remembered you pretty good," he said. "I spent some time in Cummins working with young stiffs who wanted to box. I took one look at you and figured if Tiger liked you, maybe you were okay. He told me about that fight you had once, when this guy cold-cocked you. I'm glad you made up your mind then not to do more, to get the hell out of that. You were smart. I wasn't, for a long time. Until Loutie. Anyway, when I first laid eyes on you, Shanks, I figured you had good shoulders, but a glass jaw. Drive careful."

As I backed out of Lilus Pront's driveway, my headlights shone on the pine trees he'd planted across his yard in front of the neat little brick house. A Long Line of pine trees. They were green and fresh and free, wonderfully free, in the front yard of this man who knew what freedom meant. I guess those trees said the same thing to him that they did to me that night. Free. Another kind of Long Line.

10

In Pastures Green

Shanks Caulder celebrates various holidays in various ways. Some of his ceremonies are well known, like eating turkey on Thanksgiving, shooting firecrackers on Independence Day, or turning over outside johnnies on Halloween.

Those last two, Shanks has not really done in many years, but the spirit is still there, even if the action is not.

His marking of other red-letter days on the calendar is sometimes unique. In fact, normal people don't even know some of them are red-letter days at all—like the birthday of Ezra Cornell, who founded Western Union Telegraph in the United States of America, or the anniversary of the death of Satanta, an old Kiowa chief and renegade who committed suicide by jumping off a building at the Huntsville, Texas, state penitentiary. This happened sometime in the nineteenth century. Shanks isn't consistent about the exact date. He celebrates it whenever he damn well feels like it, and sometimes more than once in a single year.

Christmas is different. Remembrance of Christmases past can bring a misty-eyed emotion rushing up. What does it is remembering when Christmas meant swirled candy and the *smell of real cedar, not red-and-green pizza and plastic wreaths that smell only like the aisles at the local Woolworth's.*

As with so many things, Shanks is somewhat ambivalent about Christmas and what it means. One year it means history, the next year soul and spirit.

But for him, the music remains constant, year to year.

I remember Christmas before the War. A long time before the War, at Grandfather's house, where there was always a big tree that he'd gone out into the hill woods and cut himself. Grandmother made popcorn strings to hang on it and everything smelled like ham and cornbread dressing. And on Christmas Eve my sisters and me would actually go to the big window in front of the living room and look out into the night sky to see if the Star of Bethlehem was there before we all walked up to the Methodist church, where Santa Claus would appear to pass out presents to the kids.

Santa Claus always had a familiar ring to his voice, like maybe he was my Uncle Jack. But I never did any sort of investigation of such a thing, because if it wasn't Uncle Jack, I'd be in deep trouble. Santa Claus scared hell out of me.

At the church, Leviticus Hammel, the preacher, would tell the story of little Jesus in the manger. Sometimes a few of the kids even listened. Not that old Leviticus wasn't a respected preacher, it was just that he did better talking about damnation and hellfire and the Old Testament than he did about a Prince of Peace and all those things.

Leviticus and Grandfather's tree and Grandmother's popcorn strings and looking for the Star was a long time ago, when I was a little kid. Then we moved to the county seat. We always came back to Weedy Rough for Christmas Eve and Christmas Day, but by then I was a big kid with a lot of embarrassing questions, and a lot more to remember about my mother's house.

Maybe memories of Christmas are more persistent than memories of any other time. Or maybe it's just because there seems to be more to remember.

Like yard lights. It wasn't long before Pearl Harbor that people had begun to hang colored lights on trees in their front yards, electric lights that had a particularly bright glitter in sharp, cold air. We'd get into my mother's 1936 Ford and drive around town, looking at them, me behind the wheel and my sisters driving me crazy yelling and squealing and screaming, "Look, look, look at that one!"

I remember then, before the War, that the kitchen in my mother's house always felt warmer than at any other time, and there were things cooking that looked better than at any other time. Sometimes in that season my mother would allow me to make fudge. And once, when the chocolate was bubbling and hissing and gurgling, my youngest sister, who was about four years old then, I guess, came in and looked at me making fudge and she saw the pot bubbling and hissing and gurgling and she asked how I made it do that. And I told her you just had to spit in it, kidding her like big brothers do with little sisters. So I turned and started chopping up some black walnut meats and when I looked back toward the stove, there's my little sister spitting into the pot of fudge.

And maybe you remember Christmas because of the important decisions, like what color necktie to buy Uncle Legette, or if you can afford a little blue bottle of Evening in Paris perfume for Aunt Bertha, or whether you ought to throw out that batch of fudge your little sister has spit in or just cook it on through to the finish and not tell anybody about it. Well, that last decision wasn't too hard because you knew damned well if you went ahead and made the stuff she'd spit in, the little monster would tell everybody about it anyway.

And I remember Christmastime before the War, when there were a lot of people around who aren't around anymore, and some who have since had the trials of Job and couldn't keep their faith like he did. Or the ones who once were pretty nice folks and somehow since have become sons of bitches, which I suppose a lot of them think applies to me.

And I remember when you could take ten dollars and buy gifts for everybody in the family. And I remember when you could listen to Dickens's *Christmas Carol*, all about Scrooge and Tiny Tim, on the radio and make up in your own mind what they looked like, which made you feel like you were a part of the creation of that story. Now all you do is sit in front of a screen and the whole shebang is laid out for you and you don't have to think or use your imagination, like you have a funnel in your head and some guy is just pouring stuff in and you just sit there with your mouth open.

But maybe most of all, what I remember about Christmas is the serenades. God, the serenades! Just the thought of them makes little ice cubes run up my back.

The best serenade of all was the last one, the last one before me and all my friends went off to foreign places to shoot at other guys. Maybe because that was the last time it ever happened, the last time that anyone even suggested it. Maybe because after we came home, we all figured there were better things to think about than serenades. But now, after the passage of a lot of time, I can't imagine what we thought was better.

But a lot of us came home after the War with different shingles on our roof, like it was proven late one night in the Gulf Café. Summer of 1946, I guess it was, and there were a bunch of us having a few hamburgers and this one guy I'd known almost all my life was there. I'd played baseball with him and honked some horn beside him in the high school band and he'd double-dated with me a couple of times when I got my mother's car toward the end of my senior year.

And this night everything was great because we were home, and then, right in the middle of eating his hamburger, this guy started crying. Not just silent crying, you understand, but wailing. And then he's up screaming about German machine guns and a buddy who suddenly didn't have any face and a lot of other stuff we couldn't understand and when we all jumped up and tried to get him quiet, he balled his fists and started hitting at us, the tears running down his face.

Jesus, a guy who'd been my friend for years, trying to flatten my nose with his fists and crying and yelling about the Rapido River and I got the idea that maybe something like going out and singing would never enter his mind again.

What the hell. The War destroyed a lot of good stuff.

But that last Christmas before the War, nobody knew what German machine guns were and they hadn't started rationing steak yet and you could still get a name-brand deck of cigarettes for twenty cents and there was no gasoline shortage. And like always, on the three nights before Christmas, we went around the town and made a serenade to various girls.

That last Christmas, we stuffed as many guys as we could get into five or six cars and drove to these houses where girls lived and we'd all pile out of the cars and sing for these girls. And that year there was snow and a full moon and I guess we looked like angels must have looked when they sang about the Coming Master, or whatever it is angels sing about. All of us in the snow, the moonlight making us a dark group in the night's whiteness, everybody with his head back and his mouth open and doing all the carols and a few things like "The Sweetheart of Sigma Chi."

Of course, the whole thing was organized by Emmy Joe Gorman, who was always organizing stuff. We'd come up the street and stop in front of the girl's house and the whole wad of guys would boil out of the cars, trying not to giggle or talk too loud because that would spoil the mood. Emmy Joe would get on the front steps of the house, or maybe just stand in the yard if it was a high terrace, so he could be above all of us and we could see him. Then he'd light a cigarette and use it to direct our singing. Like a red-eye baton, even though on that last Christmas before the war it was so bright, what with the snow and the moon, that we could see Emmy Joe as plain as if he was on the stage of the Ozark Theater, performing in the high school operetta by Gilbert and Sullivan.

Listen. It was damned good. And we knew that behind those dark windows were people listening and watching. We never sang for cookies or punch or any of that crap. And everybody in town knew it, so they never came out and offered anything. We'd just sing and then scramble back to the cars, laughing and proud of ourselves and not caring now about the noise and waking the neighborhood, and into the cars and away we went to the next girl's house.

There was one little sour note. Not in the singing, but in my feel for the whole thing.

Sometimes after the first song, Emmy Joe would turn toward the dark house and say in that loud voice that later got to be known in every courtroom in Arkansas that the singing was dedicated to Sally or Julie or Madra or whoever the hell it was who lived there, and it was sung with the best holiday wishes of Bill or Bob or Jake or some other son of a bitch, and then Emmy Joe would turn back to his choir and we'd sing the next song.

I never asked him to say the singing came with my best wishes to any of the girls. There were a lot of times I wanted to, but somehow I was embarrassed to let anybody know I thought tenderly or whatever it was toward one of those people behind the dark windows. So I'd just stand there and hear Emmy Joe dedicate the songs to some special girl from some tin-ear bastard who couldn't carry a tune in his hip pocket and didn't even know what harmony was about and I'd just sing a little louder and say it didn't make any difference.

Hell! Maybe it did.

Anyway, I figured it was all right. It's called rationalizing, I think. Because, you see, Emmy Joe never dedicated the songs from himself, either, and it was a well-known fact that most of the girls in town were straining against the screens in the open windows and freezing their butts off with nothing on but nightgowns and hoping Emmy Joe would tag his name to one of the songs being sung from their very own front yard.

But he never did.

In that whole business, sometimes a girl got left out. I mean, in a town as large as the county seat, you couldn't expect to sing to every last one of them.

So each time, before we started, we would gather at the DeLux Eat Shop and Emmy Joe would take out this little pad and pencil from under his sweater. And he'd take down all the names. The guys would suggest some names just for a joke, and Emmy Joe was very patient and he'd laugh and say that such-and-so was a very nice lady but that nobody knew all the words to "The Battle Hymn of the Republic," which was likely the only song this particular candidate understood, so she'd have to be struck off the list.

And sometimes some pretty good girls didn't make it and

this caused a lot of grumbling and Emmy Joe always settled
it by saying that if any of the present sons of bitches wanted
to conduct their own serenade they were welcome to it, and
if they did and beat us to some of the girls' houses on his own
list, every singer in this rebel group would get his ass whipped
by Shanks Caulder and other assorted bad guys. That always
made me feel pretty good.

But anyway, we'd finally get it all arranged and jump into
the cars and go charging off and sing like a bunch of maniacs
in front of the selected houses.

Then, when it was finished, we'd collect again at the DeLux
Eat Shop and have a bowl of chili or maybe a cherry milk
shake and if Deke Sanders or one of the other older guys
happened to be there, me and Emmy Joe and Pepper Winnington and Duny Jordan would drift back to the rear booth,
where one of the older guys would buy us all a bottle of Falstaff beer.

Then we'd just sit around and wait until the rest of the
crowd of serenaders would go home. Because the best part
was yet to come.

That last Christmas before the War, it was like that. And
Deke Sanders was at the DeLux Eat Shop and so was Benny
Strickler, the great trumpet man who had played with Bob
Wills and a lot of other big bands, and so me and Emmy Joe
and Pepper and Duny drifted back to the rear booth where
these two great musicians were sipping beer, and we sat down
and after a while they bought a couple of rounds of Falstaff
beer for us.

We sat there waiting for the other guys to go home, and
Deke Sanders said if somebody played Sammy Kaye's
"There'll Never Be Another You" one more time on the
Wurlitzer jukebox, he was going to puke all over the west side
of the county seat. At least I think it was Sammy Kaye.

But we waited. Because, you see, each time we serenaded
and the big bunch of guys went home, then me and Emmy Joe

and Duny and Pepper went around again, just four of us. A first tenor, a second tenor, a baritone, and a bass. And *really* sang. And the girls knew this and so did their parents, so they waited because they knew that second go-round was worth waiting up for, because that's when we really hit it. Things like "Stout-Hearted Men" and "Roses of Picardy." But best of all, a rendition of the Twenty-third Psalm. Even with just average singers, it would make the cold chills go up your back. And me and Emmy Joe and Duny and Pepper were something else than just average singers.

That second time around, our serenades were something beyond fantastic, in the deep silence of a town gone to sleep. And that year before the War, with snow and moonlight, all of us were even more inspired than ever because of the Falstaff beer those older guys had bought us, and besides that, on the night in question, Deke and Benny Strickler came along with us. Not to sing. Just to listen. And once Benny Strickler cried when we got to the part of the song that went "I'll not want."

Hell, you can't hardly want much more than that.

But there was this. The four-part harmony was so intense it seemed to make that snow a reflector that sent back echoes of each note, like we were singing in the Sistine Chapel or some other kind of holy place, and then, after going through it twice, Emmy Joe just stepped it up one-half note, changing the key, and none of us skipped a beat and did it one last time and it made the ice fall off the trees!

Well, if the ice didn't fall off the trees, it should have.

I don't even remember the names of most of the girls we sang to, but it doesn't matter now and it didn't matter then, because we were singing for ourselves. We were singing for each other. Hell, the girls were just an excuse to get out there in the cold and sing.

That last Christmas before the War, after Benny Strickler had cried listening to us, he asked everybody to come by his

house, and we did. We went in and Benny took this long
golden trumpet from a woolen sock where he kept it and he
took his mouthpiece from his shirt pocket and blew through
the horn a couple of times and then said, "Hey, men. Come
on outside."

So we followed him out to his dark front porch and he stood
there and played "O Come All Ye Faithful." I guess I cried
a little then. I don't think Emmy Joe cried at all. I don't think
Emmy Joe ever cried. He always held it in. All that holding
in killed him before his time, like there was so much there that
it finally burst.

After he'd played, Benny just turned and walked back into
his dark house and left us all there standing on his porch, so
we started going off toward home. We didn't say anything.
But after a while, me and Pepper Winnington going the same
direction, Pepper grabbed my arm and said, "Hey, why don't
you come with me to midnight Mass," him being a Catholic
and all.

So I went. It was a special time, not only Christmas but
knowing that in the coming spring when I graduated high
school, the War would grab me. So I went, and it was fantastic. Those little boys singing stuff and that preacher with a
long robe, all white and with gold figures on it or something,
and everything in Latin. And people going down on their
knees in the pews when the guy with the white robe said
something or held up this gold cup.

Man, it was impressive. For a while after that, I figured I
might want to become a Catholic. Then I realized that my
grandfather would rather I join a bowling league than become a Catholic, both of which would send me straight to
hell.

But that whole thing was getting into the feeling of Christmas. You could look at those manger scenes where they
have all these little dolls and you could think about Wise Men
bringing perfume or whatever it was they were supposed to

have brought, and all the donkeys and sheep and hogs just standing around looking at this little child.

Then there was one time at Christmas when a guy named Amos Steinmetz screwed things up. Amos was a swell kid, not very big and he never caused any trouble and he had these intense brown eyes under bushy black eyebrows, like he was looking out from under a scoop of coal dust. When we did our serenades each year, he came along, not to vocalize, you see, but just to listen like Benny Strickler did on that last Christmas before the War.

I always liked Amos. You could say something to him and he'd grin and nod his head. It didn't make any difference what it was you said. Like he wasn't going to make any trouble, no matter what, and it took me a long time to understand that it wasn't just Amos doing that, it was a long history of his people.

Anyway, I'd heard a few mothers of guys I knew saying Amos Steinmetz was of a different race. Hell, I didn't understand that because he sure as fire wasn't somebody that belonged down in the Canyon, where all the black folks lived, and he sure as sin wasn't any Osage Indian. His daddy was a little strange. He owned a big office-supply store and went around wearing a black hat and underneath that a dish-shaped skullcap.

But after one of those Christmas serenades when we were all down at the DeLux Eat Shop and guys were beginning to drift away toward home, Amos Steinmetz started pulling at my sleeve and nodding his head funny and so I went outside with him so he could say whatever it was he wanted to say. And what he wanted to say was, "Hey, Shanks, you gotta believe me, we didn't kill Him!"

Now, you talk about provincial. I didn't have the vaguest notion what this kid was talking about. I hadn't heard of anybody being killed, so I just figured little Amos had been into his old man's wine, of which, the story had it, there was a lot.

I just told Amos not to worry about it and gave him a big pat on the back and sent him home.

It was a long time later, after I'd been in the army a while and got to know some Jewish guys, that I understood what Amos was saying to me. Back in the county seat before the War, I didn't even know he was a Jew. In fact, back in the county seat before the War, I wasn't even sure what a Jew was.

And I still don't know why he was laying that killing stuff on me, because I hadn't accused him of anything. But it was like a tattoo. Once I had it, I couldn't get rid of it. All the years afterward, I kept hearing Amos saying it. "We didn't kill Him."

I figured there was supposed to be something special about Christmas and it didn't have anything to do with killing somebody. It had to do with being born. And there was Amos Steinmetz screwing up the whole arrangement for "Joy to the World."

That's right. Christmas was supposed to mean "Joy to the World" and mashed potatoes with a big glob of melting butter right on top and a sprinkle of pepper. And that last Christmas before the War, it was even more. It was the greatest serenade anybody had ever heard and it was snow on the ground and it was me and some special friends listening to Benny Strickler play his horn in the softness of the night, each note sweet and round as cotton candy, floating down off Benny's front porch to melt into the darkness.

After the War, when I came home for a little while before going back into the army, they told me Benny Strickler had finally died of TB. And Deke Sanders had got run over by a fire truck in Muskogee. And Pepper Winnington was in some insane asylum in Alabama. And Duny Jordan had been shot up pretty bad at Buna, in New Guinea. So there wasn't much left except me and Emmy Joe.

And all the girls we'd once serenaded were married to guys

we didn't even know. Not only was there nobody to go out and sing under dark windows with, but there wasn't anybody left to sing to.

Sometimes me and Emmy Joe would sit around and have a little glass of brandy from a bottle he'd liberated from Germany and we'd sing the old songs. It was pretty good. But with only a second tenor and a bass, it was nothing to compare with those old times when the four-part harmony would come crashing in on your senses when you were doing the Twenty-third and the hair would stand up on the back of your neck.

And now even Emmy Joe's gone. Sometimes when there's some snow on the ground and it's late at night, I hum a few bars of the old Twenty-third. No harmony now, of course, but I can still hear it in my head. The trouble is, nobody else can hear it. And that's the blast about it, having somebody else hear it.

Everything's got some sort of signature. And the signature for those old serenades was the arrangement of the Twenty-third Psalm. It was done by our high school music director. He was a real character, the kind one wouldn't ordinarily associate with such things as the Lord's Prayer or anything else out of the Bible. We owed him a lot because, of everything we sang, that old Twenty-third was just simply the best.

This guy's name was Dabney Judson, and he'd once been a cornet player in the Barnum & Bailey Circus. Anybody who knows will tell you, playing in the brass section of a circus band is murder. You play all afternoon in the parade and then you play all night at the performances. So this guy had an iron lip, but he was also good at writing down notes that he'd thought up himself. And he was pretty good at eyeing the pretty girls in the high school chorus.

Mr. Judson wore a homburg hat and had a Clark Gable mustache. The county seat before the war wasn't really ready for homburg hats and Clark Gable mustaches. Maybe that was part of the problem. But whatever it was, Mr. Judson had to leave because people started talking about him doing things a teacher wasn't supposed to do. Nobody ever proved anything. They just talked about it in the Smoke Shop and the Castle Lunch and at the basketball games. So Mr. Judson got tired of taking all the shit and he left. But the son of a bitch was a genius with notes, and with words to go with the notes. He would write it and guys like me and Emmy Joe and Duny Jordan and Pepper Winnington would sing it.

Now, after all these years, I dream about that singing. I can hear the chords and harmonies and the pauses and the inflections and the heat and tempo and pulse of it and I wake in a sweat because for a long minute I think Emmy Joe and the others have gone out on a serenade and not asked me to go along. They're out there in the cold moonlight, doing the Twenty-third, and Emmy Joe directing with a fire-tipped cigarette and there's breathless suspense from the folks behind those dark windows, waiting for each new figure, each new phrase, each new thundering sound.

Then I realize all of that was a long time ago and I turn over and try to get back to sleep. It usually takes a while, because I can still hear the singing. I can still see the elms and oaks that have all been cut down. I can still smell the hot apple cider. And when I do finally sleep, hoping the dream will return so I can listen once more, the dreams are always about something else. And it's gone, even in dreams.

> *The Lord's my shepherd, I'll not want.*
> *He makes me down to lie*
> *In pastures green. He leadeth me*
> *The quiet waters by.*
> *Goodness and mercy all my life*
> *Shall surely follow me.*
> *And in God's house forever more,*
> *My dwelling place shall be.*

I suppose you learn something from everything, whether you know it or not. And what I've learned from the memory of going out with a bunch of good guys and singing the old Twenty-third is that if you don't refresh your memory now and again, you forget. Because much as I loved those harmonies and those words to go with it, I have to repeat them to myself every so often or even that will be gone too. Which proves, I guess, that nothing, even greatness, is indelible.

Sorry, Mr. Judson. Sorry, Emmy Joe. Sorry, Christmas. And Amos, I know you didn't do it.